SANTA'S LITTLE ANGEL

L.M. LONDON

Formatted with Vellum

To the readers who secretly hope Santa will slide down their chimney and "rearrange" their holiday décor.

This one's for you.

Santa's Little Angel is a dark and spicy Christmas novella. This book is quite dark and sexual so please read responsibly.

- Abuse (Emotional, mental, and physical)
- Mentions of suicide (Very minimal)
- Cheating (I don't condone cheating, but after you read what happens here, you would probably swap sides too!)
- Childhood and on page trauma
- Gore, killing, death, and torture (Please be aware that I use Christmas decorations in this for purposes that aren't just for decorating)
- Eyeballs, eye sockets, and other bodily organs (Only briefly during torture)
- Sexual language and explicit sexual scenes (Again, Christmas decor is used for non-decorating purposes)
- Kidnapping and abduction
- Morally grey characters
- Mentions of organised crime

Prologue

Arlee

I KNEW my life would come to this, I have been trained for it my whole life. Cook, clean, look after the men in the house, no matter how mad or how drunk they are. It's a woman's responsibility to look after the house and her man, no matter what. But I knew the consequences of this, no friends, no help, no freedom, no pleasure for myself.

Mum spent the past eighteen years grooming me to be the perfect wife. She always said that my looks would only get me so far, even though I was beautiful. Pale skin with rosy cheeks and long jet-black hair that hangs past my ass. She knew that my looks could land me a husband but if I didn't know how to look after him that it would be a waste.

Today was the day of my eighteenth birthday, but also my wedding day. I was promised to Henry when I reached the age of fourteen. Knowing my beauty wouldn't diminish in four years, he wanted me to himself and with my family working in his illegal trade business, how can they say no.

"Come on now, Arlee. Don't look so miserable, you're going to crease your makeup." Mum smiles at me through the mirror.

I give her a fake but sweet smile to cover up my feelings, like I always do. I know today won't change much for me. My feelings are always compressed; I have never done anything I want to with my life or ever got a choice because I am made to please Henry.

Henry has been a part of my family for as long as I can remember, he's also older than me by twelve years. He was respectful in the sense that he knew not to touch me or call me his until I was eighteen. But he would hurt those who would try to talk to me or want to be my friend, leaving me with no one. Hurting any men that tried to get close, emotionally controlling my family into running his illegal guns and drugs across borders. Now, my family are all scared of him and are on tight leashes, plus with the money he offered them for me, who were they to refuse?

"Mum, for fuck sake, stop fussing so much. My hair is fine!" I swat her hands off my hair and storm away to the couch in our little suite.

The suite's ivory white with black detailing on the trims and frames, massive windows take over the wall, showing us a beautiful view of where the ceremony will be held. The black couch was so soft that I could fall asleep on it, but I have no time.

"You need to put it up, it's more elegant up in a bun or a ponytail." Mum tries to put my hair up all the time, but I love how long and gorgeous it is. If I can't cut it, why not display it.

"Leave. It." I seethe, standing from the couch and walking over to where my dress hangs. The white fabric sends an uncomfortable shiver down my spine. This is my future, the wife of an illegal businessman, with no family or help by my side.

"Okay, okay. But we need to get you in that dress now. Henry's waiting, honey." Mum's voice strains at the end of her sentence, holding back her tears as she steps beside me. "I am so proud of you, but know once you are married, we won't be here for you anymore. You will be on your own."

I know this already. Dad makes it quite clear that he's pleased to send me off for the money. I can feel the angry tears stinging my eyes, knowing that my family doesn't want me. But I don't want to be somewhere where I'm not wanted.

Mum and I spend the next thirty minutes trying to put this hideous off-white dress on my body. I was too small, but Henry wanted me to look as skinny as possible today. He says that I would never want to look back on my wedding photos and think that I look fat in them. Not that I think I'm fat, but he wants a picture perfect day and of course, being the good wife that I am, I'll do what he wants or suffer the consequences.

"Mum, I literally can't breathe." My lungs start to burn with the lack of oxygen I'm getting; stars slowly start to form around the edges of my vision.

"Well, you need to suck it up and breathe. It's time to go." She pats my shoulders and walks around the edge of my dress to frill out the edges, making it look even bigger than before. The top is so cinched that I look like I have no waist or ribs. The bottom is so fucking big and fluffy that my legs feel so naked underneath. Oh, and the frills, they make me look like one of those dolls that sit on top of the toilet rolls.

I really want to rip this off.

We slowly walk out of the room and go down the long

hallway that leads to the outdoor ceremony area. "You ready?" Mum whispers, patting down her dress with a smile on her face.

"No, but let's go." My voice is flat and unhappy, making Mum's smile vanish as I push open the doors with a fake smile on my face.

The traditional wedding song starts playing by the string band, and everyone stands from their chairs, turning to take in the sight of me in this stupid dress. The flower girls walk down first, throwing yellow flower petals everywhere and sit down at the front in their little chairs. Then, I slowly walk down the aisle with Mum, her arm locking with mine. But all I can think about is how my future is about to be taken away… and how awful these fucking shoes are!

We make it to the end of the aisle, Mum leaves me with Henry, kissing my cheek as tears fill her eyes while she sits down next to where Dad is. Dad's face couldn't be happier to see me up here with a wealthy man, knowing that he's about to get a shit ton of money.

"We have come together in the presence of God, to witness the joining in marriage of this man, Henry Kalven and this woman, Arlee Keller." The Pastor starts his speech as I turn to face him. Henry's face is beaming with pride, his aging wrinkles deepening as he looks down and smiles at me. While I am staring off into space, hoping this will end soon.

After what feels like hours, Henry reads out his vows, promising to look after me through everything and anything. Making me proud and to cherish the small moments that we will have. I force myself not to roll my eyes, I know none of this is true. He cares too much about his business and his whores to give it up for me, I am just a display wife, a trophy wife.

Then, the pastor turns to me to start mine. I try to hold back my laugh as I start to read the piece of paper Mum handed me before we left this morning.

"Henry, I promise to walk beside you through whatever life brings, to celebrate with you, and to build a future together. No matter what happens, I will stand by your side, look after you and our future children and to be the best wife I can be. I can't wait to see what the future holds for our family." Fuck sake, could she have handed me something that didn't sound so generic!

"By the power vested in me, I pronounce that they are indeed husband and wife. You may now kiss the bride."

Everyone begins to cheer and clap as Henry's massive hand reaches for my waist, his fingers reaching around the small of my back. I shudder under his touch, goosebumps spread all over me, reminding me that I haven't been touched by a man before. I look up at his face, his emerald, green eyes stare a hole into mine. Slowly, he bends down to press his lips onto mine. For the first time in my life, I am finally being kissed by someone, and... no sparks? No warm, gooey feeling? No butterflies or magical moments like Mum always said. None.

Henry pulls away and takes my hand in his, turning to face the crowd of people that are here to celebrate us. We walk down the aisle, and everyone starts cheering him on while he shouts and carries on with them. But I don't know any of them.

Instead of a big reception, Henry wants to immediately leave in a limo and go to our honeymoon in Italy. I know he has business there to handle, that's why it's our honeymoon destination. I wanted to go to Paris, but I have no say anymore. I am his to control now, not his wife, but his property.

FINALLY, we arrive on the Amalfi Coast, and I get off the plane to stretch. The smells of Italy come flooding to my nose, the smell of freshly baked items, and the flowers planted around makes my heart fill with joy. At least it's pretty here.

"You ready?" Henry whispers in my ear, sending a cold chill down my spine. I know what he means, Mum always spoke of what happens after the wedding ceremony. Not that I haven't done things before, but never with another person, I wasn't allowed to ruin myself like that.

The fantasies I've had in the shower, wishing for a tall and rugged man to make me his, make me beg. Pulling my hair and making me moan his name. After Henry had shown me photos of his crews and some of his rival crews, I couldn't get one of them out of my head. Praying that maybe, just maybe, Henry would please me enough to get him out of my head. So, my hopes are high for Henry. I've heard what he's done with other women, but I can't help the tight knot in my stomach. What if I can't perform well enough or I'm not pretty enough? Am I even enough for him? Not just for sex but for everything else?

I nod with a nervous smile and he takes us straight to our hotel that we are staying at for the next few weeks. The hotel was beautiful, the exterior was made from sandstone, looking like a massive sandcastle sitting on the water's edge. It had massive windows flooding the sides of the cream-coloured walls and the lighting underneath made it look grand! Inside was even more beautiful, the inside was all white with black detailing like my suite for the wedding, but this was more elegant. The furniture was modern but had an older feel to it, the patterns of the fabrics across the floor were something I have never seen before. Everywhere I look, something new catches my eye.

"Room of Kalven." Henry pulls out his platinum member credit card and his ID to show the younger lady behind the counter. Her eyes widen at the look of Henry. I must admit, he is gorgeous, his sandy blonde hair, with his piercing green eyes. His muscular frame has a big part to play and holds my expectations for tonight so high. The receptionist smiles and looks at her computer, and as she goes to say something Henry turns to me and basically makes out with me in front of her, proving that he is definitely taken. "Sorry, we are on our honeymoon." He wipes away the saliva that was across his mouth and takes back his cards and the room key. The girl and I make eye contact, both of us are just as shocked and embarrassed by his performance. She quickly looks away from us as she says to have a nice stay.

Our first day and night are interesting, to say the least. Henry leaves in the morning to go out for the day, sorting out business while I am stuck in the room to do whatever I please. But I can't do what I am pleased! I watch TV, order too much room service, watch the beach and waves from my fucking balcony. I cry over my lunch, realising what my life is actually becoming. But then Henry would come back in the afternoon, his dark hair would be all wild and messy, and every time I want to ask what he did, knowing full well what would have happened. But the way he looks at me as he puts his belongings on the cupboard makes my insides melt.

As soon as he closes the door to the room and kicks his men out, he starts to strip and waltzes over to the bathroom, asking me to join him.

The shower sex is… difficult. The height difference

makes it almost impossible for me to enjoy anything. Henry lifts me up, wrapping my legs around his waist and ripping my hair out of the braid I have it in. Grabbing a fistful of my long black hair, he slams my back into the freezing cold wall and immediately slides his cock into me. No warning, no foreplay, no kiss… nothing. After about two minutes, he moans in my ears and turns the water off. My skin crawls as he still holds me on his cock and carries me to bed. Though, he finally starts to kiss me, relieving the crawling sensation and replacing it with tingling in my stomach. Suddenly, he throws me down onto the mattress, making me bounce a few times before he climbs over me and takes me again. Using no fingers or words to ask if I am ready, he fucks me. He didn't make love to me, but he fucks me and hard.

My insides started to scream and ache, begging for all of this to end. While Henry breathes heavy on my neck, I would try to think of my fantasies to help me get through this. Then, when Henry is close to finishing, he lifts my hips up and digs his fingers deep into them. Making me light up inside, finally feeling him inside me. Hitting the best spot, my stomach starts to flip around and my eyes roll back, but it only lasts five seconds.

He starts moaning and cums in me, pausing his movements while he catches his breath. His fingers slightly let go of their grip holding me still so every last drop of his 'children' lands in me.

All my thoughts and feelings come crashing down, what the fuck am I doing? Is this now my life, my sex life? Henry looks back down at me and smiles, looking like he had the best time and kisses my forehead. When he leaves me to clean himself, I lay on the bed and try really hard to not cry. Is this what the next two weeks will be like? Am I his prisoner and his personal sex doll?

I HAVE NEVER BEEN SO thankful for something to be over! Our honeymoon is finally over after Henry extended our 'honeymoon' for four more weeks. As we sit on the plane, I look out the window and have a strange feeling, is the plane ride home longer than when we came?

My stomach churns tightly and nausea washes over me. I spin and Henry is busy chatting up the flight attendant. I try to stand up but the flight attendant yells to sit back in my chair, at least until we are in the air. I sit back down but I don't have time to wait. I'm about to throw up all over Henry's plane and he doesn't care! I grab one of the plastic bags beside me and throw up immediately in it, bringing up my breakfast. Great.

"Are you okay?" Henry didn't sound worried, but excited. His eyes flicker with anticipation, wondering what's wrong with me.

"I think so." I wipe my mouth with the back of my hand and realise what's happening. My stomach drops, making me nauseous all over again. Tears prick my eyes as I wait for the plane to get into the sky.

Now that I can take my seat belt off, I take out one of the pregnancy tests from the bathroom and take it, praying I am not already pregnant. I haven't done anything yet, I can't be. He knew what he was doing, only wanting sex for an heir to his business, how can I be so fucking stupid.

These are the longest three minutes of my life and I can hear Henry waiting outside the bathroom door to hear the news. I throw up again waiting, the anticipation is making me sick, that has to be it. Maybe it was the waiting around, the plane or maybe I caught a bug. God, no way! I can't be! I turn the test over and immediately break down, landing hard on my knees as I sob into my hands. Henry opens the door and sees the positive mark, his face beams brightly like it was on the day of our wedding.

"I'm going to be a dad! It's a boy, I can feel it!" He shouts, celebrating with wine and calling his Mum.

I can't believe this! What have I done?

Chapter 1

Arlee

Seven years later

CHRISTMAS IS FINALLY HERE! December first marks the start of Christmas decorating, baking, Christmas songs and my favourite thing, my daughter's birthday. Every year, I plan a huge birthday celebration for her, only for Henry to never show up. This year will be different; I will make Henry celebrate both whether he likes it or not.

"Mummy!" Gracie runs down the stairs and slams into me, wrapping her tiny arms around my stomach. I pull her in tightly, not wanting to let her go. "Guess what today marks!" She jumps off me and bounces on the balls of her feet in excitement.

"What is it, baby?" I turn to grab the bags of decorations that I know she will ask for.

"It's Christmas month, Mummy! And my birthday month! We need-"

"Decorations!" I laugh, turning with the big bags of

Christmas decorations in my hands. Her smile lights up the whole room, making my heart squeeze hard in my chest. "Now, where do you want to start?" I ask, placing them down over on the dining room table.

Gracie turns her smile from me and looks around, finding the first room she wants to conquer. She points at the hallway first and we get started. Draping colourful tinsel off the top of the wall, making it look like waves. Then we add baubles that hang from the ceiling, taping them so they hold their place and swap the carpet out to our Christmas one.

Room after room, it starts to look like Santa decorated my house himself! Different decorations are hanging everywhere, colours and lights twinkling away while Gracie stares at the amazing work we both did.

"It's beautiful, baby. Now, who wants to bake some cookies for Daddy? He will be home soon." Gracie's hand flies up as high as she can reach, saying she wants to bake the cookies for him. We race over to the kitchen and start making the cookies, batches after batches.

"Daddy's home!" Henry shouts, slurring his words and swaying around side to side.

"DADDY!" Gracie puts down the beaters she was licking and runs over to Henry, almost knocking him off his feet. "Daddy, do you like the decorations?" She asks, trying not to bust with excitement.

Henry eyes lift up from his daughter's face and looks around, his face cringing more and more until it lands on mine, I pull my eyebrows together and gesture for him to tell her something nice.

"Yeah, it's… great." He pauses, trying to not upset her. "Why don't you go get dressed, I have a surprise for you and Mummy. Dress in your cute Santa dress." He whispers, kissing her forehead.

Gracie looks over at me, the joy slowly diminishes from her sweet face. I force the biggest smile I can and nod towards the stairs, telling her it's okay. Her lips slightly flick up as she races up the stairs, leaving Henry and I alone downstairs together.

"Thank you for not being rude about the decorations, I could see it on your face that you don't like it." I whisk the eggs together with the dry ingredients, avoiding his gaze.

"Well, she's little, can't break her heart too soon. We are going to get Santa photos. I have a tip saying the competition is there. The rival gang, I don't know who will be there, but I need to scope them out." He sits at the very decorated dining table and pulls out his flask, filled with whiskey.

"Why are you slurring your words and drinking already? It's ten in the morning, Henry!" I snap under my breath, trying to make sure Gracie doesn't hear me.

"It's none of your business, woman. You are here to cook and clean, and to watch our daughter. Not to question me." He stands, slowly walking over to me, his face tinges with shades of red. I steady my heart and hold my head high; I will not back down from him.

"When you come home drunk in front of our daughter, it is my business." I snap, holding my ground.

"How dare you!" He yells, raising his hand at me. "Don't you dare talk to me like I know nothing." His hand comes down and slaps my face, the sting racing to my eye and cheek, sending water to flow freely down my cheeks. "That was just a warning, now go get dressed. Make sure you're covered up, including that new bruise on your face." He takes another swig from the flask and walks into the lounge room, leaving me there in shock.

I race up the stairs and into our ensuite bathroom to check my cheek. The welt is already appearing and is angry and bruising fast. Fuck sake. I quickly take out my makeup and cover it up, then change into the matching Christmas dress to Gracie so our photos can be cute. I can't help the powerless feeling in the pit of my stomach. The hitting, the abuse, it's all too much. He doesn't hit Gracie, thank God, but I would have left him if he did. Though, I can't just leave, it's not that simple. Being the Boss's wife in an illegal trading crew, I can't just pick up and leave without being found. I need to do something, I need to escape with Gracie and be able to hide, to be protected.

"Hurry up! We're going to be late!" Henry shouts, slamming his fist against the stairwell wall, probably putting a new hole in it after I just patched the last one.

I take a deep breath and check my face one last time, hoping you can't see the bruise. I stare at myself for a moment, looking past the bruise and down to my defenceless soul. We will escape, we will be safe, one day.

Chapter 2

Ace

God, you would think being the Boss of an illegal trading gang, someone would fucking do this shit for me. But no, everyone had to be busy today so it only left me to dress as fucking Santa Claus for the kids. My guys are lucky I have a weak spot for children and that it's only for a few hours this afternoon and tonight.

"Looking good, Boss." Talon laughed, leaning against my office door.

"You better shut the fuck up, Talon. I'll shove you in my sack if you piss me off today." He laughs harder as he walks into my office, sitting in the chair opposite from me. "What do you want?" I huff.

"Henry will be there today, we got intel saying he will be with his wife and kid." His eyes shot to mine, making me smile a little. "Though that isn't the main reason I'm telling you this though," He pauses, making my stomach drop like I'm on a fucking rollercoaster. "Henry abuses his wife, we don't know if he hits the daughter, but word is that his wife has tried to leave multiple times and was unsuccessful."

Suddenly, I could feel the rage forming in my stomach. No man should hit a woman, no matter what they do to you. We have to help, hold them here until they are safe?

Fuck! What a pathetic bitch he is! How can he even think that's okay!

"Good to know. Do we have a picture of the wife and child?" I'm hoping he says no, if I know what they look like and they do show up today, I'm going to have to stop myself from hitting Henry right there.

"We do, I sent it to your phone already." I clench my fists together, my knuckles go white as my nails bite into my skin. "Henry is powerful, Ace. He has resources and power that some may be scared of, but he's pathetic." Talon stands and takes his leave with that.

I pull my phone out of the giant fucking red pocket and look at their picture. Henry is front and centre of course, trying to play 'big man' with a professional and clean cut look. In front of him is a little girl with long dark hair and green eyes, eyes like her fathers. As I look at the woman beside him, my heart stops. I almost drop my phone looking at her gorgeous face, her pale skin looks like porcelain and her rose cheeks contrast with her jet-black hair that hangs down low to the ground. Her stunning blue eyes pierce through the phone and look into my soul, making my heart race with attraction and rage.

This lucky motherfucker has a stunning wife and beautiful kid and still beats his wife!

I stare at my phone, gripping the sides so tightly that the phone starts to crack. I stare at his smug face as he rests his hand on her hip. Her face isn't happy, it's sad, begging for someone to help. I throw my phone at the wall in rage, hoping to smash the picture of a pathetic man. I can't believe this shit!

After watching my father beat my mother to her death while drunk, I sobbed for hours over her body, until I heard a bang in the kitchen. My little legs ran as fast as they could and there he was, hanging from the roof.

He left me in the foster care system, struggling until I was eighteen. Thankfully, I was picked up from my father figure, Fang. Who treated me as his own son, like I was the only thing he ever cared about. He taught me about life, his business and how to love people who aren't family by blood. After Fang sadly passed, I started building his empire up, forming one of the biggest rings in the country. All that's left to get to the top is Henry and his company, and now I have my way in.

I get up from my desk and grab the rest of the costume, making sure I don't forget anything. My crew have been doing the Santa Claus photos for years. I hated Christmas, it was when that pathetic piece of shit took the one person I loved from me. But I have to suck it up and do it this year, no one else will.

I grab my keys and throw all my shit into the Ute, leaving the main office building and going to the shopping centre. Blasting heavy rock out of my speakers, I try to wrap my head around the fact that Henry does this to them. I have known him for years now, before he was married, and he never comes off as one to hit his wife, not that they ever tell anyone. He's been in this game for a while, and we have crossed paths multiple times at functions and… meetings. He's not once got his hands dirty during business, but I guess behind closed doors is different.

What a piece of shit, hitting someone who is weaker

than him. Thinking he's big and tough, well just wait to see what I have in store for you.

Pulling into the staff car park, I lift out the massive red sack out of the tray and fill it with a few presents the crew brought in for tonight to give the children, then I walk through the back door. I find the centre management office and see a woman, about mid-forties, sitting in the reception spot flicking through papers, not looking up at the huge guy that's standing in a Santa costume. "Hi, I'm Ace. I'm the Santa Claus for the photo booth this afternoon." I smile at her, trying to come off as nice as I can while still plotting against Henry.

"Oh, hi there! I'm Pamela, we have your spot ready, if you want to follow me?" Pamela leads me through the centre, eyes following our every step as we get to the covered area. The Santa chair I will be in for the next few hours is glorious. Soft red cushions surround the massive throne. The gold frame chair is filled with the most comfortable red fabric I have ever sat on, God this will be such a good afternoon. "Let me know if you need anything, there will be a break for you to have something to eat and we will finish at ten. Is that okay with you?" She turns to look at me, stepping back a step to look up at my face.

"That's fine by me." I drop the Santa sack beside the chair and help her set everything up for the afternoon.

Four comes around faster than expected, families started to line up at three thirty to get their family photos taken, making me want to walk out of here already. I have to do this for six hours, putting up with parents whining about their lives while I sit and only listen to their kids talk. I never pay any attention to the parents, they just want nice photos, but the kids, they want to see Santa, want to ask him about their wishes and if they are on the naughty or nice list. Luckily, all the kids are on my nice list, I am only here for them, to give them something to look forward to.

"Alright everyone, Santa is ready to meet you all!" Pamela shouts as I sit in the chair, fixing my costume up to make everything look believable. Unfortunately, I have dark scruffy hair, a well-maintained body and a tan complexion, unlike Santa who has the white hair, long ass beard and a beer gut that stops him from seeing his feet. But the suit has a fat belly built in and the hat has the fake hair and beard attached so I'm pretty convincing. "Single line please, and no pushing. You all will get a turn."

Family after family makes their way up to me, the parents waiting for their child to ask me their questions, snapping the pictures and each kid leaves with some sort of wrapped present. All being gender neutral so there aren't any issues when they open it. Then I see him, Henry. His slick back hair and his black suit, standing in line behind the next family. His wrinkled face is deep in his phone, not looking up to see who may be in front of him. Obviously not thinking his business rival would be Santa Claus. I try to look past the family in the front of the line to see if he is with his wife, but I can't see past the big bastard in front of him.

"Next!" The photographer shouts, letting the family in front of Henry move forward. Two children run up to me and jump on my lap, forcing my focus away from him and his family.

"Santa! Is it really you?" The boy asks, his face glowing with excitement. His sister is on my other knee, trying to be patient for me to answer the question.

"Ho ho ho, of course I am Santa! Tell me, what is your Christmas wish?" I laugh, trying really hard to not kill Henry with my glare as his daughter's voice flows to my ears, wanting his attention.

"I want a pony!" The other little girl's voice makes me look away from them. Fuck, she can't sit still, she's squirming like crazy, trying to release her excitement.

"I want a new game, Santa!" The boy shouts, hugging my side.

"Haha, of course. I will tell my elves back at the North Pole to get them ready for you! Now, let's get a photo for Mum and Dad." I smile through the thick beard and the photographer gets everyone in position. Taking the photo and giving the thumbs up, the kids both hug me again before running off to the side with their parents, laughing and giggling as they walk off.

Suddenly, she catches my full attention, God she's more gorgeous in person. Her stunning eyes snap to mine, sending electricity through my veins. Her rosy cheeks on her pale skin makes me squirm in the chair, the fabric of the costume becomes very uncomfortable. Thankfully, there was no rising of little Santa. Thanks to Henry being here, not that he would see with his smug face buried deep into his screen.

"Next!" Henry finally looks up from his phone and shoves his wife forward, making my skin prick with rage. I stand quickly from the chair as he pushes her, his stern expression faces me and then his brows crease. He studies me for a moment, trying to figure out if he knows who I am or not, but the costume covers almost every inch of my normal physique.

"Santa! I am so excited to see you!" Henry's daughter runs up to me and hugs my leg. I look away from him and down to his daughter, rubbing her back gently with my gloved hand.

"Ho ho ho, I am happy to see you, little one." She looks up at me and her little green eyes start filling with happy tears, making my heart swell.

I sit back on the throne, picking her up to sit her on my knee. "Now, little one, what is your Christmas wish?" I whisper in her ear, side eyeing Henry as he is deep in his phone. Not caring about his daughter or what's happening around him. His wife is in awe of her daughter talking to Santa, happy tears rolling down her cheek-wait, is that a bruise?

"Santa." The girl whispers back in my ear, snapping my rage from the bruise on her mum's face to her little pouty face. "I want my mum to be happy. Daddy is always angry at her and she cries every night. I hear her." The child's breath catches in her throat as tears fall down her cheeks. I turn fully to the girl and wipe the tear from her cheek with a gentle smile on my face. "Can you do that, Santa?" She whimpers, trying to hold back the rest of her tears.

I look at her for a moment, then turn to her mother. Her bruised eye stares straight at me, making my hands tremble with rage. "What's your name, little one?" I ask the girl, trying to calm her down.

"Gracie." She says, sniffling and wiping her eyes.

"And what's your mummy's name?" I turn to grab her the biggest present I can find in the bag and hand it to her, giving her a little hope for Christmas. Hearing your mother cry isn't something a child should hear, especially when it comes from your abusive father.

"Arlee." A trembling voice cuts in, sending jolts through my heart. As I look up, her beautiful blue eyes stare into my soul, just like the picture did. Her long black hair contrasts hard against her pale skin, making her look like a doll.

"Well, Arlee, it's nice to meet you." I purr, leaving her rosy cheeks more red than before. "Gracie, I think I can arrange for that to happen. Leave it with me, little one." I whisper in Gracie's ear. When I pull away her face is ecstatic, joy starts spreading around from me to Arlee, both of our faces glowing at the child's happiness.

"Are we ready for the picture or what?" Henry cuts in, looking bored as ever. His head tilts a little as he examines me, still trying to figure out who I am.

"Of course," I say, low and deep, hoping he may catch on so I can fight him here.

Henry rolls his eyes and stands to my side, while Gracie gets in a better position for the photo. Arlee crouches down beside Gracie and I, being as close as she can to her baby. Her perfume flies past my nose, coffee and caramel scents warm my heart. I try not to move as her hand rests on my leg, supporting her up in the crouch she's in. Her soft touch makes my stomach freak out; her hand slides up a little more and suddenly my clothes are uncomfortable again.

"Perfect." The photographer says, looking down at the camera and walking over to the computer. Henry immediately walks off to the side and Gracie watches him leave, her face drops.

"Don't worry, little one. Your wish will come true, and I may even see you soon." I whisper, her lips flick up into a massive grin. She jumps off my lap and runs over to Henry, who is death staring me now.

Finally caught on, did we?

"Thank you," Arlee mutters, trying not to speak too loudly. "She has had a rough year, and so have I. So, whoever you really are, thank you for making her happy today." She holds out her hand to shake mine. I stand from my throne and take her small hand in mine, lifting the beard from my face, I kiss the back of her hand.

"The pleasure is all mine." I look over at the line to make sure no children saw me lift the beard, thankfully no one did. I then turn to Henry who is on the phone, talking to someone on the other end with his back turned to us. "I'm Ace, I hope to see you soon, angel." Arlee smirks at me, covering her face and turns away to go over to her family. I can see the massive bruise she has on her eye and cheek. The black and purple skin trying to be concealed with a shit ton of makeup, but peeks through it all.

Don't worry, angel. I will see you again real soon.

Chapter 3

Arlee

GRACIE IS SKIPPING through the centre's halls while holding Henry's hand. My heart sinks knowing that he's not paying any attention to her, but she's happy her father is here and that's what matters, right?

"Daddy, did you like meeting Santa? He was so amazing!" She shouts, still giddy over meeting the 'real' Santa Claus.

"Yep, so great." Henry automatically said, sounding like a robot while he's scrolling through his phone.

I try really hard to not roll my eyes as Gracie turns to me, her face dropping a little. A pang of disappointment strikes me, she's also unhappy with Henry. "I need to go to the office, I'll take an uber there and you can drive the car home. I will be home later, so don't wait up for me." With that, Henry lets go of Gracie's hand without even looking at her or saying bye. Leaving us both in shock in the middle of the shopping centre.

"Daddy?" Her small cry makes me miserable. God, what is wrong with him!

"Come here, baby. Let's go get something to eat." I take her hand in mine and lead her to the food court. Her little whimpers make me want to burn the centre down, but unfortunately, food is the only thing I can do right now… and cuddles, of course.

We sit down in a private area in the little food court of the shopping centre, waiting for Gracie to settle down a little. I look around to see what we might eat, but something catches my eye, a shining light from the toilet entrance. The suspicious light is there one second and then vanishes, making my curiosity take over.

"Want to come with me to the toilet, baby?" I ask Gracie, she sniffles and slightly nods at me. She jumps off my lap and takes my hand, walking around the table and chairs to the path to the bathroom. The shining light flashes again and vanishes into the parent toilet, I know I shouldn't follow but it says the toilets unoccupied. Maybe someone needs help or needs something for their baby.

I push the button to open the door, and it looks empty. We walk in and look around, no one at the changing tables, or in the playgrounds, not even the breast-feeding room. I walk around to the toilets and suddenly everything goes dark, and I hear Gracie's cries slowly vanish.

MY HEAD STARTS to pound as my eyes squint open, what happened?

I slowly open my eyes and look around. I'm in a nice apartment with white walls and a small amount of

Christmas decorations, very minimal furniture and… Gracie?

I keep looking around, panicked that she isn't around with me, her small cries fading away from earlier replay in my head.

"Hello, angel." A familiar deep voice cuts through my quickly panicking thoughts. I've heard that voice…

Stepping around the corner, he takes in the view, as do I. His messy dark hair hangs over his forehead and his dark brown eyes peer through the strands. My mind races at the sight of this man, I know him. I have seen him in Henry's pictures of his rival gangs, "Don't worry, Gracie is safe, you are safe." He whispers, crouching down beside me. I realise that I'm not tied up or even injured, just sitting on a black couch.

"Where is she? Who are you? Where's Henry?" I stand, panic surges through me anyway. I don't know this man personally, he doesn't know me, I don't think.

"Mummy!" Gracie runs around the same corner as the man did and jumps at me, launching me back right into the couch. "Are you okay?" She checks me over, stopping at the bruise on my eye but skips over it like it's nothing new.

"I'm okay, baby. Are you? Did they hurt you?" I sit up quickly and scan her, trying to see if they touched her while I was out cold.

Gracie slaps my hands off her to stop me fussing. "No, Mummy. I'm not hurt, I was scared but they saved us." She whispers, crawling off of me and walks back to another man behind the one that's crouched down beside me. He has the same dark and scruffy hair as this man does, but he has lighter skin than him and has scars all over his body.

"To answer your questions. I am Ace, and this is Talon, we work in the same line of work as Henry, but we aren't his. I am the boss here, and Henry has no idea where you are, you're safe here." Ace's voice purrs at me, soft and gentle, similar to the way that Santa spoke.

"You're his rival he wanted to look out for today?" I slowly think about what's happening, are we really free? Henry went back to the office and- "You're Santa?" I whisper, trying to make sure Gracie doesn't hear me. She may be turning eight, but she doesn't need her heart crushed over if Santa is real or not.

"I am. Nice to make your acquaintance, angel. Now, we threw your phone out and any jewellery you were wearing including your wedding ring, so he can't track you. But I have a feeling he knew who I was and that's why he left. So, until he figures shit out, welcome home." Ace smiles at me and holds his hand out to help me up. My head's racing a million kilometres an hour as I take his hand cautiously. Ace smiles and leads me out to the hall while Talon gently takes Gracie's hand, her lips are stretching ear to ear. She must really like these guys, she usually is really shy with people she doesn't know.

We go down the hall and to the elevator, taking it down to the lobby. The elevator ride was cute, Gracie spends the whole time telling Talon and Ace about the Santa she met today. Ace's cheeks blush as she says how much she loved him and Talon tries really hard not to laugh over the compliments she is giving him.

The elevator opens and both Gracie and I gasp at the sight. If I thought our house was decorated, this was like a Christmas bomb went off! Every inch of the lobby was covered in red, green and white decorations, tinsel everywhere and baubles hanging like ours from the roof. Gracie was so happy that she runs out of the elevator and immediately joins the other kids in the decorating.

"She likes Christmas I'm assuming?" Talon laughs and

walks out, Ace stands in the elevator watching me. I can see him smiling out of the corner of my eye as he studies me.

"Can I help you, sir?" I ask, crossing my arms over my chest and turn towards him. My body immediately tenses, his eyes scan my up and down, slowly taking in everything he can.

"You can, but I won't ask yet. Come, there's something I do need to talk to you about." He holds his hand out, waiting for mine. I sigh and put mine in his as we walk over to what looks like his office. The room is slightly decorated, everything sits about knee height and is a bit out of place.

"Did the kids do this?" I laugh, covering my mouth fast to try and hold back my laughter.

"They did." He laughs with me as he sits down, gesturing for me to sit too.

"So, you say we're safe here. But how do you know we weren't safe where we were?" I ask, crossing my legs and placing my hands together on top of them. Trying to come off as professional and not scared or wounded.

"Well, one, you have a bruise on your eye where I'm assuming Henry hit you probably today. It looks fresh." The colour in my face drains almost instantly, leaving a weird tingly feeling as it drains. How can he tell? "Two, I asked around and Henry sounds like a pathetic fuckface behind closed doors." Ace's face doesn't break once as he stares down at his desk. Not from the cold and deadly look that has spread through his skin. Then he looks up at me, his eyes locking onto mine and my heart stops. It's like he can see me, finally being able to see what I have been through and what I have been hiding behind all my walls.

"I-well." I stutter, trying to find the words to cover it up, but something snaps in me. "You know what, yes he's pathetic, he's an abusive asshole that makes us look like a happy little family until we are behind closed doors, but I can handle that. He has never laid a hand on Gracie, but I can take it." I shift in my chair, squeezing my hands tightly together.

"You shouldn't have to, Arlee!" Ace almost loses his cool composure, almost slamming his hands on the desk in rage. "You are so strong, you shouldn't have to deal with that though. I want to help you, he doesn't deserve you." His rage-filled words bounce through my head, tears prick my eyes as he pushes back his scruffy hair and takes a deep breath. His muscles in his arm pulses with the movement, making my insides fill with butterflies, damn what the fuck! "I have a proposition for you."

"Mhmm." Is all that comes out, I fear if I speak I may jump the desk, straddle this man and cheat on Henry, not that it would matter if I never see him again. He's cheated on me anyway, why can't I have some fun if he can.

"You deserve someone who will care for you, who won't abuse you. I want to give you that. You are stunning and I am immediately drawn to you, angel. Not just your looks, but your soul is gorgeous. I can feel the struggle you have gone through, but I can see the love you have for your daughter and the small amount of happiness that out shines the darkness that glooms over you. I want to get rid of your darkness." Ace stands and moves around his desk, sitting on the edge of the timber desk right in front of me. He leans down and rests his elbows on his muscular legs. My brain floods with dirty thoughts and fantasies as I watch his bottom lip being bit down. "Be my angel. I will treat you like the queen you are. Give you everything you and Gracie want, deserve." His lips flick into a smirk as he leans in, his breath drags on my neck, sending shivers through my body.

"Is that right?" I whisper back, my breath hitting the same sensitive spot on his neck. Goosebumps appear on his skin, sending exciting zaps through me.

"Yes, angel." His fingers drag up my neck gently, making their way up to my cheek, cupping it softly. I lean into his touch, hoping to god I'm not about to make a massive mistake.

"How." I whimper, my body begging for more than just his touch, but I need a promise, one that won't leave me in the same situation as before.

"How do you want me to show you, angel?" His lips finally touch me, leaving a soft kiss on my neck, but pulls back as fast as it comes. "What can I do to make you feel loved? Valued? Worshipped?"

The words that are coming out of this man's mouth makes me pinch my thighs together. His words are like music to my ears, sending my heart to sing through my chest. My skin begs for more of his touch while my insides flutter under his love struck gaze.

Fuck it.

Chapter 4

Ace

I FEEL her body give into my touch and her stare is sexy, the thoughts she's having in her pretty little head are so visible through her eyes, making the feral spirit in me release.

"I need you to tell me, angel. Do you want this?' I whimper, almost dropping to my knees, begging her to say yes. "I know you don't know me yet, but without you saying yes, I can't protect you the way I want to, the way I need to." My words stagger out between each deep breath. She drags her touch down my arm, following the lines my muscles leave, then stops at the deep scar on my forearm.

"I need this, I want more, more than he has ever given me. Can you do that?" Arlee lifts her face up at me, her lips a whisper away from me that I can feel her breath on them. My dick twitches in my pants, suddenly wearing tailored dress pants seems like a massive mistake.

"I can, for you and Gracie." I sit and let her take

control, waiting for her to choose if she wants to take this opportunity and leave Henry behind, or to go back and not be able to escape the inevitable.

She pauses for a second, the cogs in her pretty head move at a million kilometres an hour, trying to choose before she makes a mistake. "Fuck it." She whispers, then her lips slam into mine, claiming what she wants, what she needs.

I quickly take action and pull her off the chair to spin her around and sit her on the desk, placing myself between her legs. Our lips clash together like they were made for each other and her hands wander over my skin, becoming familiar with every inch of me. Her hands make their way down to my pants line and she tries to take them off, groaning impatiently.

"Woah, angel." I grab her hands in mine, putting them above her head, "I said I would look after you. You sit there and look pretty for me." I smile, dragging my lips down her neck, letting my teeth sink into her skin, her whimpers igniting in my ear. I let go of her hands and look into her ocean eyes. "Tell me what you want me to do to you, angel. What are your fantasies?" I run my tongue over the angry skin I just sucked on, relieving the pain.

"Rough." She breathes, the only word she can let past her moans as my fingers graze her exposed skin as I lift her shirt up and over her head. A feral growl builds in the bottom of my throat as I lower myself down her body. Her back arches with every kiss and lick as I make my way down her stomach. One hand slithers its way around to the small of her back, bringing her closer to my lips while the other slides up her thigh, inch by fucking inch.

"Rough you say, angel." I pant, teasing myself as my hand finds the seams of her underwear, her fabric already soaked. My stomach flips while I pull the seams to the side, grazing my fingers over her folds, her hips rocking forward greedily. "Don't move." I demand, reaching over the desk to grab the leftover Christmas lights. "Let's get a little festive, huh, angel?" Her captivating smile spreads wide while I wrap her arms together with the setting lights and finish it around her hips before plugging them in. "God, look at you shine." I breathe, lowering myself to my knees to see what beauty is waiting for me.

Jesus, she is intoxicating. The sight of her being wet over me, over the teasing and the words makes my dick rub hard against my pants.

I want her, need her, desire her, she will be mine.

I slid my thumb through her and put pressure on the bundle of nerves at the top of her pussy, just enough to get a shameless moan out of her. The greed of her body takes over, needing more, she pushes against me.

I grant her wish and move my thumb in circular motions, watching as she rides my finger to please herself.

"Look how gorgeous you are." I whisper, sliding my hand down her pussy and inserting a finger inside her. Her tied up hands fly over my head, resting behind my neck, her nails digging into my skin as I push it deeper inside her. "So damn tight, angel." I watch her ride my finger, her hips moving in a fast rhythm to sooth herself. I remove my fingers, angry that they are getting all the fun, even though watching Arlee fall apart over my hand is fuelling me.

"Ace." She whimpers, begging for more. Her eyes widen as I pull my pants off, finally releasing little Santa from its very tight entrapment. She licks her lips, her imagination runs wild with all the things she wishes she could do. But for right now, she's the only one that will be pleased.

I grip her hair in my fist, taking enough to pull her

head back to expose her neck to me, "Enjoy the ride." I hum, nipping her lobe gently between my teeth.

I sink my teeth down hard on her neck while pulling her hair back harder, making her arms pull tighter around my neck to steady herself. Her moans send my dick wild, thickening more than it has ever before. The way she looks as she gasps makes me smirk, her stunning eyes rolling to the back of her head, her nails scraping against my skin. Fuck, she's going to be the death of me.

Sliding my fingers back inside her, she moans lightly as I prepare her for what's to come. My fingers let go of her hair so she can look at me, her eyes never leave mine as I plunge my knuckles into her. Her lip sucks into her mouth, holding back the harsh cries trying to escape.

"Are you sure?" I ask as I smack my lips on hers, gently removing my hand and teasing her entrance with my dick. Waiting for any sign of her to back out now, making sure she fully knows what this means.

"Yes, Ace. Please." She begs, her gasps escaping as I push deep into her. The feeling of her gripping around me makes everything vanish. Her fingertips dig hard into my shoulders, pulling me in closer to her, the lights almost blinding me. "Fuck, Ace." Her moans fuel the fire inside me, pushing deeper and deeper into her, ignoring the bright flashes of light. Her hair is still in my fist as I pull her head back hard, pushing her hips closer into me, gaining more access.

"You feel…" I mutter, trying to praise her, but I can't think anymore. I thrust harder and harder into her, slowly removing myself and then pounding against her. I slide my free hand back down between her legs, circling her clit as I pick up the pace. Her cries become more desperate as she reaches close to the end.

"Don't stop." She pants, trying to wrap her arms

around my neck again to give me full control of her body. Arlee groans in frustration over the entrapment of the Christmas lights, stopping her from getting what she wants. I tilt her hips up ever so slightly, hitting the G spot perfectly and grab her wrists to hold them over her head, stretching her out from me to see everything.

I trap her loud cries with my mouth, trying to conceal what we are doing while everyone is outside. Arlee's pussy tightens around my cock, pushing us both over the edge. My dick pulses as my streams coat her insides, mixing with her own. My knees start to shake as I pull out, dropping to the chair behind me with a smile stretching across my face.

"Wow, angel. You're stunning, you know that?" I ask, gasping for air as I stand back up, pulling her close to my naked body to hold her steady. Her forehead is glistening with sweat as I reach down and untangle the fairy lights wrapping her arms and body. What a gorgeous sight!

"That was amazing! I have never…" She stops, realising that everyone is cheering and listening to Christmas music outside the office. "Fuck, do you think they heard me?" Panic rises in her face as she jumps off my desk and throws her clothes back on.

"Angel." I stop her, grabbing her waist and bringing her back to me. I pull her into me, kissing her until her panic shifts into lust. "Just breathe. The office is sound proof, can't have everyone hearing my plans." I wink and chuckle, sweeping her messy strands out of her face. "Here, I have a mirror in my desk, you should probably fix your hair before rejoining us out here." I hand her the mirror and kiss her passionately one last time.

"What are you saying?" She laughs, taking the mirror out of my hand.

"I'm saying that you are gorgeous when you come undone for me, but no one else needs to see you like this.

That's only for my eyes now." I smile at her while she blushes at my words. "I'll see you soon, we're having some hot chocolate and singing Christmas songs, so join us when you're ready." I pull the door open and close it gently behind me. My back rests on the door for a moment as the memory washes over me again.

God, this woman will ruin me.

Chapter 5

Arlee

THE SCARED AND worried feeling of Henry taking away our freedom and happiness has finally lifted. After spending the past few days with all the families in the crew, doing Christmas preparations and Gracie making so many new friends, it makes me so happy.

Ace gave Gracie and I an apartment up on the top floor of his main building, conveniently he is our neighbour. But all the families have been giving us things that we had in Henry's house that we now no longer have. Things like clothes and toiletries, cooking stuff, groceries and so much more that I felt like we didn't deserve.

"Mummy, can I go play with Blake?" Gracie comes running around the corner and bounces on her feet in excitement.

"Of course, baby." I kiss her forehead and she zooms off, out the door to the lobby. The lobby is where most of the children play, and there are always adults there watching the kids closely, plus Talon has been assigned to babysitting duties for Gracie by Ace.

I finish tidying up the kitchen from dinner last night and make my way over to Ace's apartment next door. He has plans for Gracie's birthday apparently. I knock on his door and wait, my stomach starts to do backflips thinking back to our first time, in his office.

Now that it has been a few days, we haven't had much time to be alone while we settle in. Everyone's been so nice and has brought us food and made sure we had clothes and blankets. Which is super sweet and I couldn't feel more happy if I tried, but I have always done things for myself since Henry isn't a help but it's getting a bit much.

"Hey, angel." Ace purrs as he opens the door, leaning against the door frame. His shirtless figure almost knocks me off my feet. His hair is wet from probably the shower, but fuck me. My heart races at the glorious sight, my eyes trail down his body, not giving a care in the world about what he thinks.

"H-hi." I stumble. Fuck sake Arlee, get your shit together.

"Wanna come in? I'm cooking breakfast." He smiles, holding the door open for me. I smile back at him and nod, walking through the door and almost stop in my tracks. His apartment is decorated like downstairs, except it's nicer and not as messy.

"Did you decorate?" I ask, looking around at everything he has hanging up, he must like the white Christmas vibe, having white, blue and gold decorations up everywhere.

"I did, Christmas… it holds a special place in my heart." His words stutter slightly, before he turns to check on the pancakes in the pan.

"Well, I wanted to talk to you about Gracie's birthday,

it's a week away and I haven't been able to go home and grab anything yet. None of our stuff or the present I bought for her birthday and Christmas are here. I need to go get them." I sit down at his breakfast bar and smile at the picture of a boy and what looks like his mum hugging together, sleeping on the couch.

"I can't let you do that, angel. Henry will be there, it isn't safe and you're mine now." His voice is dark, almost demanding. I raise my eyebrows at his back, frustration settling in my stomach.

"I thought I would get freedom with you, Ace. Not being kept in captivity, behind closed doors like him." I don't raise my voice, at least I try not to, but I can't do that again. "I can't be contained or forced to do things that I don't want to do, I need freedom and love."

"I'm nothing like him!" He turns to me, his eyes well with tears and the offense is written all over his face.

"I know that, but…" I pause, trying to figure out what to do. Frustration tears fill my vision as Ace puts down the egg flip and walks over to me, pulling me into his bare chest.

"Fine, but you need to take someone with you. I can't go, but I can make Talon take you. I'll watch Gracie and see what she wants for her birthday, okay?" He whispers, lifting my chin up by his fingers. My heart starts to race and my core tightens by his gentle touch. My panties immediately soaking themselves with arousal, I just love how easily I give in now that I know what love and safety feels like.

"Okay." I whimper, melting into his touch.

"I have something for you, angel." His breath sweeping over my skin makes my skin shiver. I look down at his hand that's holding a small velvet box, the case looks small in his hands.

"What's this?" I look back up at him and his grin tells me nothing. I shake my head and look back down at the box, taking it out of his hand and opening it. I gasp, losing all the words I wanted to say as I stare down at the stunning necklace inside. The silver chain glows under the kitchen lights and the little heart pendant has three stones in it. Zircon for December, Gracie's birthday month. Amethyst for February, my birthday and then a diamond on the end for April, but it's not Henry's birthday.

"I thought instead, now that you're mine, it is only fitting I be on here with you and Gracie." He stands behind me and wraps his muscular arms around me, his hands rest at my breasts.

I turn my head and look up at him, "Thank you, it's beautiful." I hand him the necklace to put it on for me. Lifting my hair, he makes quick work of the necklace clasp as his fingers lightly press on my neck to make me face him.

"Not as beautiful as you." His lips find mine, passion flies through the air. This is rough and hard like it was the other day in Ace's office, this was soft and filled with love. His hands trail their way up my shirt, cupping my breast in one hand while the other flips the bra hooks a part in one flick. Fuck, that's hot.

"Do you want breakfast?" He leans into my neck, planting kisses and bites on my neck, making me moan under his touches. I shake my head at him, not being able to think of making words right now.

Ace smiles against the skin of my neck, his lips grazing me gently. His hands wander down my body and scoop me up from the bottom of my thighs, walking us over to his bedroom. Giggles escape my lips as he places me down on his mattress, watching me as my breasts bounce from the fall. His eyes darken with possession as he lifts his gaze to mine.

"Do you have time for me, angel?" Ace's look weakens, taking in the sight of my half naked body. Tracing every line and groove like he is mapping it out in his mind.

"Do you?" I tease, enjoying the view of him watching me, wanting to have what he thinks he can't have. His breath stutters as I slowly reach for my waist band, shimmying it down painfully slow, not leaving his sight.

"Angel." Ace moves closer, reaching to touch me. But before his hands can lay on me, I put my foot out against his shoulder, halting him.

"Mhmm, we need to plan some things today, Ace. Plus, I would like to speak on some… things as well." My voice lowers as I slip my pants off my leg, letting Ace remove it from the other that is at his shoulder.

"What is it?" He demands, his hands itching to have more than my leg. He runs his hands up my calf, kissing my ankle, then my calf while his hand follows up my thigh.

"Gracie's birthday. Me getting my stuff from Henry's-"

"Do not speak of his name while you are almost naked on my bed, angel!" Ace seethes, digging his fingers into my inner thigh. I beg the moan rising in my throat to not reveal itself. "I'm sorry, I did not mean to hurt you." He rushes up off his knees, staring down at my bruised leg.

"No, Ace. Please don't be sorry. I liked it." I bite down on my bottom lip hard, blood trickles down from the cut, leaving a copper taste behind. "But we have to be quick, we have a busy day today."

"I will try, but I enjoy taking my time with you." His shit-stirring grin spreads wide on his face as he reaches under the bed for something. Tinsel?

"Ace?" My tone comes out more questioning than it

should, we already went through this with the fairy lights, why would it be any different now.

"Yes, angel? What, do you not want to have some fun?" He breathfully laughs, shaking his head as he stands. "Move to the middle of the bed and spread out." His demanding voice leaves no room for questions, I move and hold my arms and legs out wide. He hums with approval as he ties me up to the frame of the bed. "Stay still." His voice doesn't shift from the demanding tone as he lowers his eyes to my core. His glare lays thick over me, staring down with greed and dominance as it swirls in his dark brown eyes. My clit aches as I watch him, locking onto his gorgeous body. His tanned skin shimmering in the morning sun and his abs and muscles twitching with need.

I watch him as his stare sears me as he drops down in front of me, kissing each side of my legs and each section, little by little. My ankles, my calves, my knee, then to my outer and inner thighs. My core tenses and my heart pounds in my ears, I want more, I need more!

Ace looks up at me through his messy hair, running his tongue up my inner thigh and over the fabric that stops his touch from soothing the aching the fire inside me. I close my eyes and focus on his touch. The way his breath hits the sizzling in between my legs, the way his fingers trail over the seam of my underwear, the way his tongue pushes through the fabric and rubs it over my clit.

"Ace!" I stutter, sliding my hands through his wet hair, fisting it in between my fingers. His gravelly laugh shakes my core while he moves the fabric aside and slams his tongue inside me. Licking and nipping at every part of me, sending shocks of pain through me. His tongue runs over my clit, circling the nerves and then his mouth stretches over me, moaning against it. I close my eyes and arch my back into the pleasure in between my legs, hoping for more, desperate.

"God, getting greedy, angel." Ace says against me, sliding his massive fingers inside me. I stare down at him, his dark eyes peering under me, full of lust and desire. His fingers curl in me, hitting all the right spots while I slowly melt into the mattress.

"Ace, I-I'm…" A wave crushes me, his fingers and mouth pushing me over the edge. Stars fill my vision as he continues his work until there is nothing left for him to clean up with his mouth.

"Close, I can see that." He laughs, standing up with my cum on his face.

"You have a little." I say, pointing at my chin to show him where it is, my cheeks start flaming with embarrassment. The tinsel shines in the morning sun, creating colours across the walls.

"Don't be embarrassed. You taste so good." He crawls on top of me, grabbing a shirt to wipe his face clean. "Now, we have some plans to make, do we not?" He asks, untying the colourful decorations and holding his hand out for me.

"You're not… We're not?" Confusion drowns me, is that it? Does he not want anything from me in return?

"Do you want more? You came, that was the goal. Now, I'm starving." Ace smiles at me as I try to understand that not everyone needs pleasing apparently. "So, do you like pancakes?" He returns to the stove, shirtless, thanks to me.

"Yeah, I'm still confused. Do you not want sex or anything in return for that?" I sit down at the bar again.

"No, do you want sex? We can have sex if you want but I don't expect anything in return for pleasing you, angel." He hands me a plate stacked with pancakes he must have made before. “Sorry, they may be a little cold now.”

“No, it’s okay. Just, that’s never happened before. Anyways." I say, trying to shift the conversation. “Gracie’s birthday, I like to keep it separated from Christmas. So can you find out what theme she wants and any presents she would like?. I want to go over to Henry’s today. He shouldn’t be home.” I cut up one of the pancakes and shove it into my mouth, almost moaning at the fluffiness of the cake. “Holy shit!”

“They are good, right? It was my mum’s recipe. One of the few things I have left.” He pauses looking down at my plate with a sad smile. “But, I can find that out for you and Talon is going with you. I will call him and tell him the plan. Eat and then you can go get ready, you look beautiful, but I think if Talon sees you like this, he may blush.” Ace chuckles and kisses my forehead. I check in the camera of my phone and mascara is running down my face and my lips are swollen from me biting at them.

Fuck sake.

Chapter 6

Arlee

"THIS IS A BAD IDEA, he probably has the house guarded, waiting for us to come home!"

"Don't worry, Arlee. We have done a sweep of the neighbourhood and have men standing by, just in case. Henry isn't here." Talon assures me, smiling at me as he drives down my old street.

Memories come flooding back of my time here. The times he hit me, kicked me, even locking me outside because I was being a 'bitch' and 'bitches sleep outside'. No one came to help me, no one cared enough to do anything, all because they knew Henry, or they worked for him.

But that's not the case anymore. I am safe and have people who care about Gracie and I.

We pull up on the street, next to the house. Our Christmas decorations outside are still up. The tinsel hanging around the poles and the star on the roof. The blow-up Santa and snowman are still holding their place on the lawn and the door still has the Christmas wreath on it.

"Are you ready?" Talon asks, making sure I don't want to turn back. Even though I want to, I need my stuff and so does Gracie.

"Yeah, let's go." I smile, trying to hide my nerves as I open my door. We walk along the driveway and knock on the door. Even though Ace's men checked to see if anyone was home, we are still checking.

After what feels like forever, no one comes to the door, nor is there any noise coming from inside. Talon nods and unlocks the door with a lock pick. I know we don't have a security system so there isn't any stress for that as we walk in. I immediately stop as I scan my beautiful home, but the place is a fucking disaster.

The Christmas tree is thrown across the living room, all the tinsel that was hanging on the roof is now torn and thrown everywhere, even the baubles have been smashed into tiny pieces.

"Wow." I whisper, walking around the mess, trying to see if someone was still here or not.

"He is really a monster, isn't he?" Talon questions as he follows my lead. I don't answer him though, I'm only focused on getting mine and Gracie's things and getting the fuck out of here.

"Go upstairs, go left and the second door on the right is Gracie's room. Grab as much as you can, I'm going to start with the presents that are still here." I demand, trying not to cry at the disaster Henry made after he realised we weren't coming home.

Talon nods, moving past me and up the stairs. I walk over to the kitchen and grab a big rubbish bag, needing something big to fit all the presents in. I don't even make it back to where the tree was when I hear a massive bang from upstairs.

Talon.

I drop the bag and sprint up the stairs, skipping every second step. I turn hard and trip as I get to the top, running to Gracie's door and shoving it open. Talon is on the floor, motionless and blood everywhere, but no one is here.

"Talon…" I breathe, running and dropping down beside him. His eyes are lifeless as he stares at the wall with Gracie's bed against it. "Talon! No, no, no, no. Wake up, Talon!" I shout, shaking his body in hopes he's playing a prank on me.

"He's dead." A voice slices through my panicking cries, making my heart stop. "And you're coming with us." Footsteps become louder as I turn.

"No, please." I beg, trying to stand but instead I fall to the ground, a massive sting forming on the back of my head.

MY HEAD POUNDS with pain as I slowly flutter my eyes open. The pain makes me nauseous, making my head spin around the room. I try to look around at where I am, but everything is tied up. My arms, legs, body, even my fucking neck.

My body tenses as footsteps approach from behind me, "Finally, feels like you have been asleep forever." A familiar voice scratches through the dark room. "I've missed you." Henry steps out from the shadows, his face looks rugged with his stubble growing in. His green eyes are dark and hollow from what looks like no sleep and his clothes are creased and messy, nothing like the well-kept man I once knew.

"What do you want!" I shout, trying to squirm out of the rope that ties me down to the chair. Every fibre is slicing into me, irritating my skin.

"You, and Gracie of course. I just want my family back." Henry sits down in front of me, placing his head on my lap and wrapping his arms around my legs. "God, I have missed you so much, Arlee." His voice breaks as a tear leaks from his eyes onto my pants.

"Get off of me." I seethe. "You didn't miss us! You missed having people to control." Red fills my vision and the rage builds low in my stomach.

"No!" Henry shouts, pushing up off my legs to stand tall over me. "You are mine, you are all I have. Where did you go? Who was that with you?" His face twists into a snarl, his dominant energy radiating off of him. "Have you been fucking him, huh?" He huffs, stepping closer to me. "Have you ruined yourself?"

"I haven't been fucking him! Did you kill him?" I ask, but Henry's hand is all that answers me, swinging down and slapping the side of my face. A loud snap passes my ears, followed by the eerily silence. A white hot flash spreads across my skin, tears flow down the numbness on my cheek. I sit there for a moment, taking in what just happened, how can this be happening again. I look up to hope that Henry is shocked from it as well, after being away for a while but Henry's face is flat, and full of fury.

"Bullshit! You have been fucking someone if not him, who!" He pushes me back hard, my chair scraping against the wooden floor until I hit hard against the bricks. "You want to know if he's dead, tell me who you have been fucking then."

My vision blurs as I shake my head, trying to get rid of the numbness of my cheek. "You want us back? But you haven't changed! You just hit me, Henry! You shouldn't hit your wife!" I spit, blood leaking from my mouth as I lower my head. "You want to know who? Fine. It's Ace!" I shout, trying to rip out of my restraints. "He took us from the shopping centre after the Santa photos. He's kept us safe, protecting us, he looks after us, after me. The way a wife should be looked after!" I stop, noticing that Henry's expression still hasn't changed.

The cogs above his head turning as he processes what I'm saying. His rival, I have been with his rival the whole time and he hasn't found us.

"Your turn! Is. He. Dead." I whisper, trying not to hurt his feelings anymore, knowing how fragile his ego can be.

"Yes, Arlee. He's dead, we only knocked him out to get you, but once my men grabbed you, we didn't need him. So, they beat him to death with what they could find, happy?" Henry's smile was atrocious, something the devil himself would be scared to look at. I twist and turn in the chair, attempting one more time to free myself. "You know what, maybe I'll go give your little boyfriend a gift. Just to show him that you are returned back to your rightful owner." He stalks over to me, a glimmer of a blade slices over my head. A soft crunching sound fills the room and my head suddenly feels lighter as I hear my long hair falling down to the floor. "There, let's see how he feels without your gorgeous hair." Henry runs the blade over my jaw line, lifting my head to face his. My heart beats so loud that I can feel my shirt moving with it. "I will get back what's mine."

"Wait until he finds out what you have done, Henry." I snarl, overcome by anger and sadness of my hair being to my shoulders for the first time ever. "Once I'm free, I will kill you with my bare fucking hands!" I promise.

Henry stares at me for a moment before a laugh erupts from his lips, turning and leaving me alone while someone comes in to grab my hair and leaves. The cold and dark room encloses me, leaving only the thoughts of Gracie being safe with Ace and no matter what, he will protect her.

Chapter 7

Ace

IT'S BEEN over two days since I last heard from anyone, my skin crawls as I pace through my office. We have spent most of that time looking for them, for my men, for Talon and Arlee, but nothing. They just vanished!

I watch as Gracie and the other kids in the building decorate the tree, throwing tinsel and fake snow everywhere, baubles bouncing all over the place and the laughter that follows. If only they knew how bad the real world was, if only someone could prepare them for all of this without them having to find out on their own. I won't do it though, I can't break their precious hearts.

"Ace. You need to see this." Ninja almost breaks my door off its hinges as he storms in, huffing and puffing like he ran a marathon.

"What?" I follow him out, past the children and out the front door. My mind stops racing as I look at the four-wheel-drive parked out in the front car park, a black Patrol with heavily tinted windows so we can't see the inside. "How long have they been here?" I ask, trying not to slap Ninja and Guard right there for even letting unwanted visitors into my car park.

"They just got here, sir." Guard halts beside me, standing at ease due to his military training. "No one has stepped out of the car either. We don't know who it is or what they want." His voice coming out flat and well trained, not a hint of feeling.

"I know who they are, look at the number plate. It's Henry's crew, something's wrong." I whisper, walking past both men and stopping at the edge of our perimeter.

The car doors finally swing open, men come out from both sides of the front of the vehicle. One of the men, Trick, is short and stocky, with dark buzzed hair and a scar that goes down the side of his face. One that I gave him years ago for the foul words he said to me at one of the *meetings* we had. The other is a taller man, Savage, he has dirty blonde hair with blue eyes and wears an ugly fucking yellow trench coat everywhere.

Savage slams his door closed and turns to open the back, a black dress shoe appears from under the door, followed by another. Savage bows as Henry walks around, holding a bag of something in his hand, almost dragging it on the ground.

"Ace, what a… lovely place you have here." Henry grimaces as he takes in the view of my main apartment building. The rage in me is already building as he steps closer to the perimeter.

"Thanks. What the fuck are you doing here, Henry?" My voice carrying across the parking lot, loud and frustrated. My limbs threaten to shake with rage as he steps closer to me.

"Oh, I have something of yours that I thought you

would like back." Henry's smile is spread from ear to ear, but not with joy. This… this is something else. He holds up the small black rubbish bag up above his head, waving it in the air like he was teasing a dog with its toy.

I nod to Guard to grab it from him, flicking my head at the bag in Henry's hand. Guard nods back at me and paces over to Henry and the bag

"Oh no, Ace. You should come get this. It is a gift for you, of course." Henry holds back the bag out of Guard's reach, laughing and shaking his head at him. Guard turns, watching me as I walk over, making sure neither one of us kills each other right here.

The small rubbish bag in his hand dangles above his head, trying to tease me more and more with it.

"May I remind you, Henry." I hiss, standing toe to toe with this disgusting *man*, "I am taller than you, and quite stronger." I snatch the bag out of his hand as he huffs at my chest. My vision starts to blur with wrath as I look down into the bag. "What. Is. This!" I say, almost startling myself with how calm the words come out through my teeth.

"A present." Henry laughs, taking a step back to ensure his safety.

I reach into the back and instantly pull my hand out in disgust. The contents inside makes my skin crawl, something familiar to the touch but something that shouldn't be in a bag. I reach in again and take a fist full of the smooth and fine… hair!

"Wha-what have you done?" My eyes can not look away from the gorgeous midnight black hair that I have in my hands. I watch as the strands fall between my fingertips and my hands are on the verge of trembling.

"Oh, but there's more." Henry's voice tears my thoughts apart as Trick opens the other side of the car, dragging out someone from the back. The body is wrapped in a body bag, dead.

"I am getting sick of your fucking presents, Henry. I don't want a dead body, but you will explain this right fucking now before you join that body." I stomp forward, only to be stopped by Ninja, his hand resting on my shoulder.

"You will want this back, though. This is actually yours to begin with." His wicked smile breaks free again. Trick smiles back at him and unzips the back, pulling the top apart. My eyes almost pop right out of my head at the sight. My heart races as I drop the bag of hair and slowly walk over to the body.

His body is completely covered in blood and his head is bashed in all different way. Not a single sign of life is left in Talon's eyes. My eyes start to water, kneeling down to my best friend's body. He's gone, no heartbeat, no breath, nothing. My brother… is dead.

"Now that I have returned what is yours, I want what is mine back." Henry once again slices my thoughts and memories in half like they do not matter, like my brother who lies dead right in front of him doesn't matter.

"Did you do this? I will fucking kill you!" I race to my feet and lung at Henry, his face doesn't change from the hideous smirk on his face as I throw my fist at his jaw. Except, it didn't smash into him, but into Trick. Motherfucker.

"I did. Take this as a warning, Ace. This is what happens when you take and fuck what isn't yours." Henry's eyes look past me to the doors of my building. I follow his sight and see Frank with Gracie, tears streaming down her face and hiding behind his leg. "Gracie, honey!" Henry pushes past me as I stand in shock, what the fuck does Frank think he's doing.

"Henry! Stay away from her!" I yell, snapping out of the freezing shock and rush to grab him before he can touch her. She doesn't deserve this, this pain, seeing him here. "She won't leave with you." I say through gritted teeth. Ninja races to my side and Guard knocks past Henry and straight to Gracie, pushing Frank out of her grip and taking her back inside. The faint whispers of him promising her that everything is okay shatters my heart.

"She isn't yours, Ace. Neither was Arlee, but I have her back now. Though her hair would be a good remembrance gift for you, considering you would have touched it, I don't want it." His face glows with red, anger sizzling off his sweaty forehead.

"Want to know what else I've touched on your pretty wife, Henry. I will get her back." I step closer to him, knowing that I can't hit him is really pissing me off. I will burn the world down to get her back, I don't care who we lose or who dies, but she will come back to me.

"Pff, sure you will. Not that you know where she is." He laughs in my face, spit flying onto my cheeks.

"We will see about that." I turn away from Henry to face Ninja, "Get Talon, put him in the back please. Have Doc meet you there and do not let anyone see him." I whisper, the words almost coming out as a plea.

My brother is gone, and the woman I thought I could protect is gone, not to mention all the men I sent out to protect them are probably gone too.

What have I done?

Chapter 8

Arlee

I DON'T KNOW how long I have been down here for. The rope has cut through a few layers of my skin, making them irritated and itch with pain. No one has come down to check on me, to feed me or to even let me go to the bathroom. With the sound of water dripping on the floor, I haven't been able to hold my bladder. My heart aches not knowing what's happening, whether Ace knows about Talon, if Gracie is safe.

As I slowly fall into a downward spiral of thoughts, the metal door swings open, hitting hard against the brick walls.

"You're still breathing, that's good. Fuck, it stinks in here!" Henry storms in, his nose scrunches up at the sheer smell I have left.

"What do you think would happen when you leave someone tied to a chair, Henry! What was I supposed to do?" I quietly shout, my words coming out harsh enough to get a side eye glare from him.

"I have come with news, we will be moving you. To give you a room at my new building." He doesn't even turn back to look at me, not another word as he leaves me. "Make sure she's clean before you move her." He mutters to the guards outside my door before leaving with them.

"Henry!" I shout, "What about Gracie?!" I cry, trying to find out anything about my daughter. Hoping he didn't get her from Ace, but there was nothing, no answer, not even a fucking sigh or grunt in response.

I struggle against the rope again, trying with whatever strength I have left to snap the ropes, but it's no use. "Fuck!" I mumble, heart breaking tears flow freely down my cheeks.

Footsteps move closer to me, their feet slapping on the cement floor. Both guards have made their way to my side, looking at me with no feeling, like they had been possessed to follow whatever they were told. I look up to the one on my left, his tall and bulky figure stands tall over me, a daunting feeling presses hard against my chest. His eyes are almost black and his lips are twisting into something sinister.

"Hi there, can I help you?" I ask, bowing my head pretending to show respect.

"Actually, you can. Sit back for me and shut up." His words are hard and demanding, making me follow them immediately.

His smile reaches ear to ear as his hand glides into my greasy short hair, cupping the back of my head. Shivers flow through me as he fists my hair and rips my head back, while the other guard, who I can barely see, slams something over my mouth. A sweet and pleasant smell overcomes me, making my head spin and my body feel heavy. My eyes flutter open and close, fighting against the drowsiness and my stomach knots so tight that I want to gag.

"Sleep well." The taller guard smiles, his words coming out like a slur and then everything again goes black.

Chapter 9

Ace

"WHAT THE FUCK HAPPENED?" Doc rushes through the doors of our back room, which has been turned into the medical bay. His hands fly around as he quickly grabs everything that he may need in case Talon could still be alive.

"That won't be necessary, Doc. He's gone." I collapse to the chair at the side of the bed, pain and fatigue washing over me. After spending days trying to find these two, and it was right under my nose this whole fucking time.

"What happened? Does Arlee need attending to?" Doc's head spins around the room, searching for anyone else that may need help.

"No, she's not here." My voice cracks as tears cover my cheeks, "I couldn't protect her. It was a simple mission, and… I've lost them both." My head drops into my hands, shaking away all the pain that lays over me like a weighted blanket. "I had one job! I-I…"

Doc comes up to me and kneels beside me, placing his hand on my shoulder. The slight comforting feeling does nothing to crack the torturing pain that hangs over me. I couldn't keep them safe. One job, I had one fucking job.

"It's not your fault, Ace. Remember that. You have done so much for everyone that we all know how much work you have put into everything. She is alive, right?"

I haven't even thought of the possibility where Henry was kind enough to let her live, after sleeping with me, her hair being cut off because I touched it. I thought maybe… he was cruel enough to kill her.

"I have her hair, he cut it because I touched it." I sniffle, clearing my throat and wiping away the tears of loss for my family. "I assumed he killed her, but…" My thoughts run wild, trying to track every last word Henry said while I was blinded with rage, hoping something slipped through the cracks.

"She isn't yours, Ace. Neither was Arlee, but I have her back now."

He has her, and she has to be alive if he wants to dangle a carrot like that in front of me. "She's alive." I mutter softly under my breath, Doc's smile makes more tears form in my eyes.

"Then, it looks like we have to go and get her." Doc pats my shoulder as he stands back up. "I will organise everything for Talon's funeral, he would want you to get her back. He loved her and Gracie, we all do." I nod at Doc and walk past him, up to my best friend's body. His pale skin slowly loses its colouring after being dead for a while, his cloudy eyes are filled with the pain and horror he would have had after being beaten the way he was. I slide my hands gently over his eyes, pulling his eyelids down with a slow swipe. My heart beats hard against my chest as if it was trying to reach him and provide for him.

"Thank you, Doc. Please tell me if you need anything. I want the best for him. Whatever you need." I whisper, holding his shoulder gently in my hand. Begging to God or Jesus, or anyone who is listening to take care of my brother.

"I will give you a minute to be with him alone, I will get the men ready for whatever you need." Doc's steps vanish out the door and the click of the door closing sends my emotions in full drive.

I stare down into his face, hoping that for some miraculous reason, he would open his eyes and come back to me.

"I'm so sorry, Brother. Why would they do this to you?" The tears return, streaming down my face as I move around the table. "I will murder him, I will make him pay for this." My knuckles turn white around the bed frame as I lean over his body. Fury and angry tears overtake the sad tears as they burn down my face. "I appreciate everything you tried to do for her, I know you protected her the best you could. You did well." I take his hand in mine, his hand limp and cold. "You can rest now, Talon. I will miss you so much. You were one of the best things that ever happened to me. You will always be my brother, blood doesn't matter." I gently place his hand back down by his side, taking in his face one last time before covering it over with the sheet.

I wipe my face of all the tears and snot as I walk over to the door. I grab the handle and pause, not wanting to leave him on his own, to cross over the line on his own. Then I remember the one thing he wanted.

"I will make sure that your name is visible to your family if they wish to see you again, James. You were always enough, goodbye." I give him one final nod and open the door, closing it gently behind me, not that it would wake him from his death sleep.

"Are you okay, Ace?" Doc pushes off the wall where he must have been waiting for me to finish saying goodbye.

"No. I'm not, but I will not wait around and let Henry take another person I love from me." I demand, realising that I have never said that I love her, to her or anyone.

"You love her?" Doc's voice isn't shocked in the slightest, he has a small smile on his face and his head tilts to the side as if he could read my mind and knows.

"I-I do. Is everyone ready?" I ask him, wiping my face one last time of the sticky streaks that remain from my tears.

"They are." He nods, walking past me and grabs the door handles and pauses, "Go get her and bring her home."

Chapter 10

Ace

I PREPARED THE MEETING ROOM. It's located on the first floor of the building where the office manager would sit if this was a real hotel. I pull out everything I know on Henry and his crew, all their details, real names, real address and all. I have been collecting shit on him for years, so one day I could finally take what is his and be at the top, but I don't want that anymore. My business is thriving being second, I have a hold of a couple higher up officers in my grasp and I was happy. Until he took it all from me, it's not the business that has my heart anymore, it's them. Talon always had a special spot, ever since we joined and made this empire, but Arlee and Gracie have the rest. It's the only thing I care about.

"You needed us, sir?" Guard walks in with almost all the men on his heels, lining around the wall of the room, trying to squeeze in to hear what's happening.

"Yes. Before we get started, I have some devastating

news to share with you all." I pause, hesitant to tell everyone about Talon, hoping they will mourn but still be able to focus, as he would want us to. "On the mission to get Arlee's and Gracie's things back from Henry's, we were ambushed, we lost a lot of men. I have no information on any of their whereabouts, whether Henry disposed of them or we were infiltrated with spies. I have no clue, but we lost one of our leaders that day." Everyone fidgeted with the news, spies in our crew was one thing but for some to vanish was another thing. "Talon was beaten to death by Henry's crew. He has been dead for days and we are unfortunately too late to do anything about it. Doc is planning his funeral arrangements."

Everyone's mask slips, no longer the hard men that we have all trained ourselves to be when we are needed for a mission. But now we are vulnerable, tears fall down some's cheeks, others dissociate from the present, all trying to understand the news.

"How bad?" Kash asked, his breath shakes as if he wants to ask more but can't.

"It was bad, I…" My heart starts to race again, the fresh memories of Talons beaten in face appear in my vision. The blood and bone that was out for the world to see, the bullet hole in his forehead that was to make sure his life was properly ended… I shook my head. Clearing the thoughts away, I need to focus, he would want me too. "He died doing something for me, something that I know any of you would have done. The little girl downstairs has no mother right now, she was taken. He was only trying to protect her, to bring her back safely."

The men all wipe their faces and stare at me, waiting for what orders I may have. "We are ready to help, anything for Gracie." Guard declares, everyone muttering in agreement. God, she really has won the heart of these rough men.

"Okay, here's the plan." I lean forward on the table, opening up notes and folders of everything I have. I even pull Ghost in, our hacker, to find out where Arlee is through the necklace I gave her. Hopefully Henry didn't notice it around her neck.

We spent most of the afternoon planning and discussing issues, trying to find places he may go with her until Ghost found her. At an old warehouse in the middle of the outback, in this fucking heat. Would she even be alive still?

"I want everyone to study everything, work out a plan and come back to me with what you have. I have to go break that little girl's heart."

GRACIE and I walk into my apartment, I didn't want to tell her about her mum while everyone is around. I grab her little hand in mine and make our way over to the couch. Her gorgeous green eyes scan over my apartment with glee, looking at all my Christmas decorations.

"Wow, Ace! Your apartment is so pretty." She breaths, her jaw almost dragging along my floors.

"Thanks, little one. Come sit on the couch." I pat the spot on my dark couch next to me, hoping that I can provide her with enough comfort.

"Okay!" She squeals, running over and jumping up on my couch. Her little head nuzzling into my side. "What's up?" She asks, hoping that it's about her birthday in a few days, but instead of celebrating, we could be mourning.

"It's about your mum." I whisper, brushing her dark strands from her face. My blood boils at the sight of her long dark hair, identical to her mothers. I'm not angry at her, but at Henry, cutting her hair like that.

"O-okay." Gracie hesitates, her fingers fidgeting together. Her eyes move fast around the room, waiting for the news.

"She's… she's back with your dad."

"What?" Her voice is so quiet that if I wasn't already looking at her, I wouldn't have heard her.

"Your dad took her back. We are going to get her back though, Little one. I don't break my promises." Her eyes are misty with tears covering them. She looks away from me as she tries to process the information.

"Does he want me back too, Ace?"

I take a minute before responding, trying to make sure I don't scare her or make her upset. I take a deep breath in and back out before looking back down at her sad little face.

"He does."

"I don't want to go back, Ace. Please don't send me back." Gracie begs, her hand is squeezing mine, pleading me not to send her away. I know she has found her family here, that she feels safe here. She knows her mother loved it here too, finally getting the happiness she deserves.

"I will never send you back, Gracie. Okay, I promise." I pull her into me, cuddling her tightly and not letting go. "We will get Mummy back okay? We are leaving soon to go get her, you will stay with one of the families here. Whoever you want." I pull her off me, but she won't let me go. She has her grip tight around my shirt and I can feel her shoulders shaking. Her breathing quickens and little sniffles follow.

"O-okay." Her muffled sniffles make tears fall down my

face. I have never known love like this before. She's not even mine and they haven't been here for very long, but they have made their way into my heart. Being the family that I never knew I needed, the child that I never thought I would have.

"Hey, I have a present for you." I whisper, wiping her tears off her cheeks. Her face finally pulls off of my shirt and her eyes are bloodshot from her crying, they scan around again, looking for something she may have missed.

"A present?"

I nod at her with a small smile. Standing off the couch, I watch her as I walk around the chair and over to the spare bedroom I have decorated just for her. One day hoping they would want to move in with me, hopefully that day can still come.

"Come here, little one." I hold my hand out, hoping she will come and want to have a look. Even though she just got one of the hardest pieces of news for a child to comprehend, she climbed off the couch and walks over to me.

"What is it?" I take her hand in mine again and open the door to her room, turning on the light to show her it.

The walls are painted with black, red and green with specks of gold through it. The painted walls are designed as a Christmas background, there are pine trees standing all along the walls in black, with red and green baubles and lines through it, imitating tinsel. Then there are gold stars and little angels on top of the trees. The sky is painted as if the night sky is always present, it's dark blue with gold glittery stars all over it. And on the roof is full of stickers shaped as snow flakes. In Australia, it never snows at Christmas time, as it's summer here, but they are a cute addition.

She moves her eyes off the walls and to the decorated

room. Her bed is a white double bed frame with Christmas sheets on it, and she has her own little personal Christmas tree to decorate. A white desk and chair to match her bed sits by the door and her belongings are sitting in the drawers after some of the mums helped me finish the project.

"This is your room, if you want it of course." I tell her, trying to hide my goofy smile, trying to not think about who helped me put it all together. It was his idea, he wanted to show her but…

"It's amazing!" Gracie shrieks, hugging my leg so tight it might cut circulation. I laugh and hug her back with my hands.

"I'm glad you like it, but there's a present on the bed for you, look." I point the massive box on the bed. Her eyes open so wide and a little gasp slips from her lips as she lets go of my leg. Gracie runs up to the bed and pulls the present down, a small thud sounds as it falls.

"Can I open it now?" I nod and before she even lets me speak, she rips the wrapping paper off and gasps so loud. "ACE! You got me a massive teddy bear!" She attempts to pull the bear out of the box but it's so big that it took both Talon and I to stuff it into that tiny box.

"Here." I chuckle, coming over to her and pulling it out for her. Her smile melts my heart as she examines it, then she pulls it in and cries into it.

"Thank you so much." She whimpers, "I want to live here with you, Ace."

"Okay, little one. First, you have to stay with someone else for a bit. I have to go get Mummy. You can take him with you." I smile at her massive smile on her face. She cuddles the bear and nods at me, though her expression changes.

"Ace, can I ask something?"

"Of course, little one." I crouch down in front of her, so she can ask me face to face.

"What's your real name? Talon told me that you guys all have code names, to help hide things from the past. I want to name the bear after you, if that's okay?" Her face begins to turn red, and she hides her face slightly into the bear, obviously knowing it's not common for anyone else but family to know someone's real name.

"Mmm," I hum, pretending to think about it. I put my finger on my lip and look around, I was planning on telling them anyway. "I guess that's okay.. My real name, it's Hunter. Nice to formally meet you, Gracie." Her cute smile floods her face and she stands quickly, dropping the bear.

"Hunter? I like it!" She says, holding out her hand as if we have never met before, "Nice to meet you properly, Hunter."

I shake my head and laugh at her. God, this kid is so fucking cute. I place my hand in hers and shake, finally able to call her my family.

Chapter 11

Arlee

WHY THE FUCK do I keep waking up in different places, I swear once I found out who these fucking idiots are, I will come for them.

I look around the new room I'm in, not that there's much to look at. The stone walls have a small amount of decor on them, a few pictures and some Christmas decorations are scattered across the wall. I try to look closer at the pictures, but the chair I'm tied into doesn't let me even wiggle.

"Finally, you're awake, my love." Henry's voice sweeps away the hazy fog in my head, instant rage and anger fuels my body.

"Where the fuck am I, Henry?!" I ask, the words barely making it past my gritted teeth. I watch him as he stalks around me, looking me up and down like I'm a deer in a lion's sight.

"Why would I tell you that? All you need to know is that you are somewhere where no one will find us." He smiles at me like nothing has changed, like the tinkle of love I had for him was still there. "All that is left now is for Gracie to join us."

"Where is she?" I cut him off, I don't care about anything else, I just need to know she's safe and not with fucking Henry. She's only safe with Ace.

"She's with your lover." He stops, his face starts to mirror my anger. I can feel my heart race like it used to, when I was scared of him. But I know that Ace is coming for me, he surely is.

"He isn't my lover, he's kept us safe. Away from you, we were finally free and then you…" A lump squirms its way through my throat, making me unable to finish my sentence. Henry twists around in an inhuman way, his head snaps straight to mine, almost a full one-eighty. I can't help the anxious feeling in my heart, begging me to move or do anything, to remove myself from the danger.

"Then I what, Arlee?" He asks, swivelling his body around to face me and steps up to me, pulling my face into his, nose to nose. "I took back what was mine. I will make you mine again. I hope you enjoyed your fuck buddy." He moves his face closer to my ear, grazing his lips over my ear, sending my body in a spasm. "You are mine." His teeth scrape my lobe, gently scraping down my neck and kissing the track his teeth made.

"Henry, please." I beg, trying to shift out of his grip, but his hands dig into my arms, holding my body still.

"God, I love when you beg for me, Arlee." His breath coats my neck, making the hair on my neck stand. He slides his hand up to cup my cheek, then pulls his face to be in front of me, "I will be back for you. When I come back, your lover will be dead and we will celebrate," He pauses, the smile on his face becomes sinister, "In our bed." He forces his lips on mine, trying to get something out of me. The taste of stale alcohol coats my lips, forcing tears to my eyes.

He grunts in approval of his torture and turns, leaving me in this basement on my own. My thoughts fly wild, he just forced himself on me. It isn't the first time, but I never thought it would ever come to this. I didn't think I would ever have to put up with this again, just my luck.

I look around the room to find something, anything to help me escape from this fucking rope. The fibres of it cut through my skin as I shuffle the chair around, my skin screaming at me in pain. There's nothing, just a dark room, with only the chair, the rope and me.

"Fuck." I mutter to myself, the gnawing feeling of hope fading away slowly. Tears streak my face as realisation settles itself in my head, I can't escape. I have to sit and wait for something, for someone to come get me. I'm hopeless, I can't do it anymore. I can't fight, I can't think that I can escape my reality, the one my parents forced me into.

Flashes of my past shoot past my vision, the day my parents told me I would be marrying a rich man, the warm and happy feeling I had knowing I would be secure. The day I actually met Henry, his handsome and well-rehearsed smile stretching over his gorgeous face. His eyes burning holes in me, the way he held himself made me so excited to be his. Then my wedding day came, my eighteenth birthday, and the honeymoon. Already knowing his true colours, not thinking he would hit me, but I knew he was in an illegal business and that he hurt people. Then the day we were coming home passed me, the day I found out I was pregnant. The only reason I stayed breathing, pushed through all of this.

She will always be safe with Ace, he will protect her and keep her away from Henry. Be able to provide her with a life that I couldn't give her, he will make a great father to her.

Chapter 12

Ace

EVERYONE'S READY, piling weapons and gear into the cars. Everyone's muttering to each other, making sure we have everything, reiterating the plan so they are all on the same page. My chest burns, my heart races knowing that Arlee is in danger, has been for days, and I made her wait.

I storm to my office, slamming my door behind me. I can feel the heart ache coming and tears follow like I commanded them to join the party. I lean up against the door, trying to breathe all of the bad thoughts of Arlee being hurt out of my head. The thought that he could be touching her, making her his again, leaving bruises on her and throwing her around like she's a fucking rag doll.

A gentle knock on the door startles me to my feet, my hands flying to my face to wipe away my tears of anger. "Come in." I grumble, clearing my throat as I walk around to my chair and sit.

"Sorry, Ace. I know you're worried. We will get her

back." Guard says, closing the door behind him. "We are all here to back you, and her. I remember first meeting her, and her daughter. The way you and Talon watched them both, but the look was always different. Talon did it out of obligation, but you…" Guard's voice cuts off as he looks up at me. His face drains of the colour as he takes in my expression. I can't hide my feelings anymore, Arlee destroyed all my walls, the walls I have had up for years and now…

"Don't talk of her as if she's gone, Guard." My voice comes out in a low and dangerous tone, making him stand from his chair and simply nod. "Let's go, she's counting on us." I stand and follow Guard out of my office.

I will burn everything for her.

EVERYONE FOLLOWS Guard to the location Ghost found for us to start looking. The necklace is still around her neck as Ghost noticed it had been moved to somewhere in the middle of nowhere. He's trying to hide her from me, but I will find her, always.

We have been driving down this dirt road for what feels like hours until we find an abandoned warehouse, the one Ghost spoke of. The outside looks almost completely broken. The wooden building has fallen to pieces, the roof half collapsed into itself, the windows are all boarded up and the front door is a simple plank of wood that looks out of place. Too new for the old building.

We stop a while away from it, to keep out of sight of Henry and anyone he has guarding the area. We have to act casual, driving past it as if we aren't suspecting a thing.

"This is it. I can feel it." I whisper, turning to look at Guard. He looks at the building, taking in all ways we can get access to it.

"We have to keep moving, we can't stay here." He says, driving on, past the building and up the road so we can set up our plan. Being ready for anything.

All the other cars come up, one by one, in different time intervals to make it look like it's just normal traffic. While the building is in the middle of nowhere, the road that the warehouse is on is a side road from one of the busier dirt roads. So, we knew that we wouldn't look suspicious if we did it throughout the day.

The sky finally turns dark and everyone has made it to the meeting spot. All of our gear piled into what is definitely needed and things that are just a precaution. Our night vision goggles lay on the backseat of one of the cars while we check all the weapons that we will be using to rescue her.

"Okay, men." I demand, everyone stops doing what they are doing and looks at me, all determined to get Arlee back to us. "I won't bore you with a long speech on how much she means to me, but if you fail, I will kill you. We won't be leaving without Arlee, either get her back or be killed doing it, understood?" Everyone mutters and nods at me, knowing that it would come to this. "Good. Now, do we all understand what to do and know where your posts are?"

We brought twelve men, each of them with a specific task. Four of them will go first, to take out the guards outside of the building. Knowing full well Henry would want her guarded at all times because of me. Then, once they are taken care of, they will take the clothes of the men and pretend to be the guards, so nothing looks out of place. Ghost will have all the cameras frozen for an hour, that's all the time we have to get in and get out. After they do their part, another four will go in and clear the building, killing anyone in their path. Henry won't be here but two of our men here will leave and go get him, with Ghost's help. Guard and I will then go get Arlee, bringing her home and straight to Doc, who is preparing for her to come back in the worst case.

Everyone grunts at me and takes their place, starting the clock for her rescue.

HALF AN HOUR INTO THE MISSION, my men killed the guards and took their clothes, but we lost one of them in the cross fire. The other four men went in almost immediately after the first four cleared outside, taking out the men inside. I can't see inside yet, but I am still waiting for word from them to tell us it's clear.

I sent the two men to go get Henry when Ghost messaged me with his coordinates, he was hanging out at his house. I am also waiting on the all clear from them.

"Ace, we are clear." Ninja's voice cuts the silence like a crack of thunder. Both Guard and I immediately start moving. While Guard gets the car and brings it to the side of the warehouse, I will go in and get Arlee.

As I step onto the front lawn of the warehouse, an engine revs loudly, spinning up dust from the road. I turn, knowing that it isn't Guard in our car, but a smaller and faster car.

Henry.

Suddenly, more cars come screaming up the dirt road, sending my men into a panic to protect me, pushing me inside. Ninja and his four men sprint out, telling me to go get Arlee while they take out Henry's men.

My heart races in my chest, the pressure making my vision blur at the edges. All my men, they could die, I would lose everything. All my family, my friends of so many years. Sounds of bullets flying shake me awake, the thoughts hammering at my head, the choice tearing me in half.

Arlee or my men.

Chapter 13

Arlee

FAINT SOUNDS of guns make my eyes open heavily. My sight flickers in and out, and my head pounds loudly, begging me to close my eyes forever and not wake up.

The sounds of screaming and guns grow louder in my ears, sending a jolt of fear through me. Has Henry come back with men to kill me? Is Ace here to rescue me? Is his men dying on my behalf?

I sit up in the chair, my limbs are numb from the rope cutting my circulation off, being wrapped so tightly around me and my jerking movements earlier didn't help. I sit and listen, waiting to hear something, anything to tell me what is actually happening. But nothing comes, I can only hear the sounds of pain and loss.

My eyes flicker close again, becoming almost too heavy to open. I can't handle this, I am okay to go knowing Gracie is safe. Knowing Ace…

The metal door swings open, making a clang sound as

it hits the stone wall. My body jolts upright and my eyes fly open, only for them to fill with tears instantly. My heart sinks hard in my chest and my vision blurs more and more as the man walks up to me.

I can't see who it is, what they want or if they want to hurt me or not.

"Please, please. I beg you not to hurt me. I just want to see my baby, please." I beg, my words slowly slurs into nothing as my body finally gives in, not being able to handle being awake anymore.

ACE

THE SOUNDS of bloodshed and screams torture my brain. My family, they're dying, there're so many of Henry's men. We are severely outnumbered. How did he know? How did he find out we were coming? Did my men get him or did he get us first?

"Fuck!" I shout, the decision tears through me like lightning through a tree. I look back through the front door one more time, watching my men slowly fall to Henry's men, my heart ripping into two. Then, I turn and run through the warehouse, trying to find the spot of a basement or a door to a room that she might be in.

My mind races through everything, searching for a door. Where could a basement be? Will she be alive still? Will this all be for nothing? Am I about to break that little girl's heart, to tell her that her mum…

"FUCK OFF!" I shout at my own thoughts, angry tears hiss down my face. I run to the other side of the building, my eyes frantically searching for fucking anything, any signs of her!

I stop and spin to check if I missed something, but then something flickers for my attention. A set of stairs covered over by debris of the building, the stone stairs glitter in the moonlight from above. My body freezes for a moment, taking in that this could be it. Knowing that Henry tried to hide the stairs from me, thinking I wouldn't notice, moron.

"Arlee?" I whisper, sprinting back to the covered stairs. I grab all the wooden planks and throw them out of the way. My legs feel heavy as I hurry down the stairs, but I pause at the door.

I have to prepare myself. She could be dead, hurt or even okay. But I need to get her out, no matter how she looks. Her daughter deserves that, I deserve that.

I push the door open hard, slamming it against the stone wall and there she is. Her head wobbles on her shoulders, "Please, please. I beg you not to hurt me. I just want to see my baby, please." Then her head drops down and her eyes slowly fall closed.

"Angel!" I shout, rushing to her side and lifting her head in my hands. Her eyes don't open again, her body is completely limp in the chair. "No, no, no." I repeat, quickly untying her from the chair. The sounds of shooting no longer register in my head, only that she is breathing, "Come on, angel." I place her down on the cold stone floor, placing my head on her chest and look at her neck, checking for a pulse. Her heart is barely beating and her pulse is weak. "Fuck, GUARD!" I shout, lifting her up in my arms, cradling her into my chest as I heave her up the stairs, praying that she makes it.

Her body is covered in angry slices from the rope cutting into her skin and the back of her head is bleeding, her black hair now tinges with red in the moonlight.

"Ace!" Guard's shouts stream through me as I turn and see him at the back of the warehouse. His face is full of worry as he sprints up to me, taking her legs in his hands while I shuffle her down and carry her arms. She's not heavy, but I am exhausted from stress and her whole body is limp.

"She's not going to make it. What-what do I do?" A lump in my throat catches on my words, cracking my voice and tears fall onto her forehead as I stare down at her.

"Ace, we need to get her in the car first." Guard's firm voice calms me a little, giving me a little hope she will make it. I nod at him and we quickly move through the warehouse to the back.

We make it out to the car and thankful my men have held back Henry's guys long enough to let me get Arlee to the car. Guard swings the back door open and places her legs up gently on the seat before letting them go and racing to the other side.

"Breathe for me, angel. For Gracie." I beg her, watching her expressionless face not move even at the words of her daughter. My stomach clenches, bile rises to the back of my throat while the feeling of failure washes over me. I had one job, I gave myself one job, one fucking promise. Now, I could be breaking that.

"Okay, here we go." Guard grabs her legs from the other side of the car and drags her in while I lift her up. I hold her head and shoulders up as I slip under her, placing her head on my lap. "Let's get her to Doc." Guard jumps in the driver's seat and drives off. Leaving all my men behind to fend for themselves, they all knew what may happen and I know they would do it again for me, for her. "Is she breathing still?" Guard looks back in the rear view mirror, looking at me and then back at the road.

"I… umm…" I wipe the frustrating tears away and place my fingers on her throat, checking the side for a pulse. I hold my breath while waiting for even a small amount of movement. A faint pulse claps against my fingertips, relief washes over me and the tears stream back down my cheeks. "Yes, she-she's got a pulse. But it's weak." I sniffle, trying to be strong for her, but the thought of losing her. I can't, I can't think like this.

"We aren't far, just hold on, Arlee." Guard speaks to her and then plants his foot on the pedal. Speeding up down the road to get us back as fast as possible.

"Hold on, angel. For Gracie and I, please." My fingers graze her cheeks, pushing her short stains of hair out of her face. Her hair… it's so short. "I will make him pay, we will make him pay!" I promise, knowing I will keep this one, no matter what happens.

Chapter 14

Ace

"DOC!" I scream, pushing open the car door and pulling Arlee out into my arms. "Where is Doc!" I shout, racing her to the treatment room, where Doc has the door pulled open.

"Here. How's she doing?" His voice is even and calm from working in this field his whole life.

"She's alive, but her breathing is almost non-existent and her pulse is thready and weak." I breathe, placing her on the gurney and then collapsing into the chair beside her. My legs are numb from the stress and exhaustion washing over me. Guard bursts through the doors and immediately comes up to me.

"Ace, you need to rest. Please, at least sleep. Gracie will need you." He holds out his hand to help me up but I slap it away. Rage gnaws at my heart and I can feel the guilt building in my stomach.

"I will not leave her." I seethe, sitting up in the chair.

"I'm staying here until she's breathing better." My eyes fall heavily and darkness encloses me like a blanket.

MY EYES FLUTTER open as Guard and Doc talk amongst each other, and a female voice makes my whole body wake up. I sit up and look around, my heart pounds hard against my rib cage as I see her. The short hair sitting right at her jawline, her rope burns cover almost half her arms and her neck, her face is hollow and bruised from a fresh hit.

"Angel." I whisper, standing up from my chair and slowly walk up to her. Scared that if I move too fast she will run away or vanish into thin air. "Is it really you, are you okay?"

"Hi, Ace." Her soft voice fills my heart, and I drop to my knees in front of her. I can't help it, tears flow freely and I start sobbing. I pull her gently into me, wrapping my arms around her lower back as I place my head into her lap. "I'm here." Arlee's hand strokes my hair and brushes it out of my face.

"I'm so sorry, I'm-"

"It's okay." Her assurance makes more sobs rip through me. I can feel her little giggles as she bends down and kisses my head. "I'm okay, I'm here and I'm okay, Ace."

I lift my head up and take her in. Her glowing aura has returned, her smile is small yet it takes over my whole heart. Her stunning blue eyes have their sparkle back and her porcelain and bright skin has slowly come back to colour. The sight of her makes me completely speechless, I don't know what to say to her. How to tell her how sorry I am for not protecting her, for leaving her and not going with her, for… fuck.

"Angel, I…" My mouth dries and my words fade away to ash. I have to tell her, tell her about him. I slowly push myself up and wipe my face, clearing my throat. I look over at Doc and Guard, who are standing over by the door.

"We will give you a minute." Guard nods and both men walk out the door, waiting to hear when they are needed.

"What? What's wrong?" Her smile fades as I turn back to her. The loss of my brother sits heavy on my chest, like I'm being crushed by a boulder all the time. I have to tell her, she and Gracie both liked him. God, he was around as much as I was.

"Angel," I take a deep breath and sit down beside her, taking her hands into mine. "Talon's gone, angel. He was beaten after they took you." I catch the crack of my voice and sit in silence, looking at her face change from confusion to pain.

Arlee's heartbroken tears break my heart, her ragged breath makes my stomach drop. She turns to me and drops her head into my chest, bawling into it. I wrap around her tight enough that it won't hurt her but so she knows it's okay. I hold back my tears, letting her get everything out on her own, letting her process what's happening while I'm strong for her.

After some time passes, she sniffles the final tears away and looks up at me, her bloodshot sapphire eyes begging me to take it back, to tell her it's not true.

"Does Gracie know?" Her raspy voice snaps something in me, anger and revenge radiate off my skin. Henry has taken so much from not just me, but from both girls. I have been selfish to just think of me, my brother, but no. It's not just me he loved like family, these two have made room on all of our hearts and now, he's gone. They don't get to see him ever again like I did, to say their goodbyes. All because of him.

"She doesn't. I didn't want to tell her anything until I could bring you back to her." I rub my thumb over her tears, collecting them off her skin.

"So, she's safe?"

"Yes, angel. She's staying in my apartment." I smile at her, cupping her face in my hands as she starts to cry again. "I know I didn't do a good job of it the first time, but I will protect you and her. I will burn him and his world down for what he did." My voice holds so much promise, so much pain that he caused. I will take everything he loves and make it mine.

"Ace?" Her questioning voice makes my eyebrows pull together in confusion. "I want to kill him." I shouldn't have, but the smile that grows on my face is dangerous.

I have always looked at Arlee as the angel that fell from heaven, the person that can make the good in me shine, but now… now she might be a devil in disguise that brings the bad out in me.

"First, we have a birthday to get to." I kiss her forehead and hand her some clothes Guard grabbed for her. A long sleeved shirt and jeans, to help hide the pain Henry caused her.

Chapter 15

Arlee

ACE GRABS my hand and opens the door to his apartment, and my jaw hits the floor. The apartment is decorated with so much Christmas stuff that it looks so enchanting, like a house directly out of a Christmas movie.

"Ace, I thought you were going to keep them separated!" I look at him, anger pumps through my veins, but his expression doesn't change. The pride and happiness in his face melts away the anger.

"I know, but when I asked Gracie, she said she wanted a Christmas themed party. She and I decorated and then some of the mums in the building continued while I came to get you back. There are party games but Christmas style and everything." He looks around with the biggest smile on his face, not a care in the world for Henry right now, just that my little girl gets exactly what she wants. Something Henry never cared for or wanted to do.

"Hunter!" Gracie shouts, running over to Ace and

cuddles his leg. "You're home! Did you…" Her eyes open wide and her mouth drops to the floor as she looks past Ace's leg and at me. Her green eyes mist over and her bottom lip quakes at the sight of me. "Mummy?" Her little voice instantly fills my heart, tears sting my eyes.

"Hi, baby." I whimper, falling down to my knees and opening my arms for her. She lets go of Ace and jumps into my arms, sending pain through me from the rope. I ignore it, not giving a care in the world about anything but her. Her loud sobs deafen my hearing, but I hold her tightly, scared to let her go.

"You're here." She pushes off me and looks my up and down, checking that I'm real and not a figure of her imagination. "You came back."

"Only because of Ace." I smile and look up at him, his face is full of happiness and sadness all at the same time. I can see the pain he has gone through to get me back, to be here for Gracie, but he looks happy to be here.

Gracie moves in closer to me, her breath reaching my ear. "His real name is Hunter, Mummy." Gracie giggles and runs back to Ace, I mean Hunter? What?

"Thanks for that, little one. Go, enjoy the party, we will be there in a sec." Gracie looks up at his face and then at mine. I give her a nod of approval and she runs off giggling to her friends.

"So." I stand back and look up at the face of the man of my dreams. His dark eyes look down at me, while his eyes look all over my face, not being able to find the right spot to sit. "Your real name isn't Ace. Henry told me some crews have nicknames to cover their identity but Ace is a real name. So, Hunter is it?" I tease, grabbing his hands in mine and stepping up on my tip toes, kissing his lips gently.

"It is. I got Ace because Lucifer was taken. I am the

best at what I do, angel." His low voice sends goosebumps over my skin, making my inside spark with excitement.

"I like it, Hunter." The teasing smile sends his dark eyes even darker, the possessiveness kicking in. His hands slither around my waist and his nose reaches down and touches mine.

"I'm glad I have your approval, angel." His lips grazes mine, making me crave for more. My body shutters against his touch, his hand reaches for my cheek, barely touching me. "Just so you know, we are at your child's birthday party. Keep it in your pants." Hunter laughs, kissing my forehead and placing my hand in his.

I roll my eyes at him and follow him into the lounge room where the party is. Gracie is glowing in the centre of it all, her Christmas dress shining in the sunlight and all the children are laughing and dancing around her. I look around and see all the different party games set up: pin the star on the tree, a bauble pinata and chairs spaced out of musical chairs, one of Gracie's favourite games.

"You did all this for her?" I whisper to Hunter, still wrapping my head around his real name, let alone all the stuff he has done for my daughter.

"I did, with help of course. We have a village here and all the mums were so excited to help. Gracie knew exactly what she wanted." He watches me soak it all in, the cheering, the laughter, all the kids and parents having a blast. I know that Gracie is an organised child but god, she is amazing. "I want to show you something." Hunter's voice tickled my ear, making me fidget under his words.

He leads me over to a room in the apartment and opens the door, flicking on the light. The room is decorated for a child with the massive Christmas theme spreading across every inch of the walls.

"This is the room Gracie is staying in, Talon and I..."

He stops talking, trying to hold back his own pain and checks me to make sure I was okay before continuing, "We decorated it for her, I wanted you two to stay with me immediately, but Talon wanted to do some decorating first. Gracie grew on him fast."

My heart almost explodes knowing that he loved her so much. Knowing that he wanted to have something special for her and for both of these men to take us into their care. Showing us the love that we never had makes me want to melt on the spot.

"I can't believe this." My words barely come out as a whisper as I scan my surroundings. Walking into the room, my fingers graze over the painted walls and look up at the snow flakes on the ceiling. He did this, they did all this for her…

"Is it too much? Too early? If you aren't ready to move in with-"

"Hunter." I cut him off, laughing his name as he panics about if he's moving too fast. "It's beautiful and I would love to move in with you." I turn back to him and cuddle into him, nuzzling my head into his chest. "You both did an amazing job, thank you." I can feel his breath stagger at my words, thanking both him and Talon.

We hold each other for a while before Gracie screams out that it's cake time. We both giggle and walk out of her room, our hands intertwined together.

We spend the rest of the afternoon watching everyone shower Gracie with love and presents. I watch as everyone cares for my child in ways I didn't know other people could, it has always just been me watching and caring for her. Now, she has a massive family and so many people that would do anything for her.

Chapter 16

Hunter

"ARE YOU READY, ANGEL?" I ask Arlee, pulling her into me like she might run away from what she is about to see.

"Well, I'm a little tired from the welcome back you were giving me." Her cheeks blush over while her fingers climb up my stomach, touching each ab through my shirt and then sliding down each groove in my arm. "But yes, I'm ready."

"Ladies first." I open the door and gesture for her to go in first. The sound of muffled cries sends excitement through me, like electricity running through my veins.

I close the door behind me and turn to look at Arlee, her short hair has grown on me now, caressing her jaw line and her skin has fully come back to life with some… nourishment. She circles around the chair that holds Henry, the same way he had her wrapped up in those fucking ropes.

Arlee rips off the hessian bag from Henry's head, his eyes squint open at the sudden light hitting his face. I spent this morning decorating the place, hanging Christmas lights and tinsel around the room, getting a Christmas tree down here and hanging baubles and candy canes from it. All for him, just so we can have some fun.

"Hope you're feeling festive, Henry. I thought out of the kindness of my heart, I would give you something pretty to look at while I slowly kill you." I say, gesturing to all of the decorations around the small room. "Oh, but want to know what the prettiest thing is in this room?" I whisper, getting really close to his face. The horror in his eyes set my heart on fire, I have been waiting for this day for so long.

"Hi, baby." Arlee purrs, walking around from behind him, her smile is anything but heavenly.

Henry groans something through the tape, not that we can tell what it is.

"Let me get that for you." She says, ripping the tape off hard and fast.

"Fuck!" He shouts, working his jaw around to ease the pain and stiffness. "What the fuck are you doing, Arlee? I am your-"

Arlee's hand raises high above her head and swings across Henry's mouth. The slap echoing in the room like thunder and an angry welt of her handprint already appears on his cheek.

"Do not finish that sentence. I am not yours anymore." Arlee seethes, walking over to the chair in the corner and sits, looking like she is the queen she is.

"Are you feeling festive yet, Henry?" I turn around to the table on the edge of the room, looking for my first piece of decor to put on the tree. Arlee hands me my Santa hat, the same one from our first moment together, just to get into the feeling. "Thank you, angel." I kiss her hand

and rub the back of it with a smirk, her cheeks heat at the small interaction.

"Can you kill me now, fuck sake. You cheating whore!" Henry shouts, spitting all over the place.

"Come on now, Henry. That's no way to speak to her." I tsk, grabbing one of the baubles and pulling off its string, knowing I have other plans for this string. "But, I guess you can keep talking, or at least try to." I turn around and pry his mouth open, shoving mouth gags into it. "Hey, angel. Change of plans, can I have the knife and the string please." Arlee hums and hands me the exact things I want, standing close beside me to watch.

I turn back to Henry, his eyes are so wide that I could just scoop them out with my fingers, but that will come. I reach in his mouth with my gloved hand and rip his tongue out, holding it steady for me to cut it.

Henry starts to fidget around, moving his head and swaying all over the place.

"I got it." Arlee sings, moving around and places her fingers on both sides of his head, holding him still. I nod in thanks to her and slice his tongue off quickly and tie it to the bauble string. Henry screams rip through the cell, making Arlee slap her hand hard over his mouth, getting the scream to stop.

"Wow, what a great decoration this will make for you." I shake my head and walk to the tree to place it on one of the branches, watching the wet flesh swing. "You're going to look so festive that it will look like Santa ran over you with the sleigh and left some of the presents behind." I laugh, not being able to help myself. Another muffled scream rips out of Henry while Arlee's hand is still over his mouth. This feels so good, it's been a while since I have tortured anyone.

"Do I get a turn, Hunter?" Arlee's arms are crossed

over her chest, pushing her tits up. Her bloody hands leave marks on her arm from having it over Henry's mouth.

"If you keep doing that, no. I will fuck you right here." I murmur, my voice coming out huskier than it meant to.

Henry screeched in disagreement, almost making us both laugh out loud.

"At least he can't speak now." Arlee shrugs, walking in front of him to assess my work. "Oh, I have an idea! His eye can be a bauble!" She jumps up and down, clapping her hands together like an excited school girl. As she turns her expression drops at my face, which is a little confused. "What?"

"Nothing, I just never thought of you as dangerous or anything but an angel. Hence the nickname." I laugh, trying to not roll on the floor.

"That's what happens when you think someone's innocent when they aren't, right, Henry?" She bends back down, her head tilts slightly at her own question. Henry's eyes are filled with horror, not realising the actual danger his 'wife' poses.

"Well, I don't think we have enough baubles on the tree and I think his *beautiful* green eye will make a perfect addition to my new favourite tree." I slide the carving knife off the table and hand it over to Arlee. "Do the honors?" I ask, dropping to one knee and holding the knife high above my head to her, like I'm presenting something to the queen.

Arlee laughs and takes the knife. She flips the blade back and forth, checking it out until she is satisfied with how it looks. She leans in close to his face, trying to get into the perfect spot to carve his eyeball out. "Stay very still." Arlee whispers, trying to focus on the task at hand.

As she leans in, I look down past her and see Henry's face, his expression changes and he goes to move, thinking this is the perfect opportunity to escape. I can see his toes lift his front chair legs off the ground. Motherfucker's going to try and headbutt her. I quickly move from behind Arlee's shoulder to around behind him, holding the back of the chair down in place.

"Nice try, fuckface. But I know this trick." I mutter, looking down at him and his face is full of madness. His skin heats, turning his flakey white skin red. His neck veins pop out in a furious strain, making them pop out so far that a knife can easily prick it and he would bleed out.

I watch as Arlee waits patiently for us to finish our lovers quarrel before she quickly takes the knife and jams it hard into his socket, making a pop sound.

"AHHH!" He cries, trying to pull away from the knife. But it was too late for him.

With another pop sound, the eyeball falls out with ease, right into Arlee's hand. I give him a hideous smile while she shoves the bauble connector into the organ. The wet tearing sound fills the room, making Henry squirm.

"Oh, sorry, does that make you uncomfortable?" Arlee laughs, raising an eyebrow at him as I get up and add the eye to the tree.

I stand back to admire our work, hands resting on my hips, but I feel like something is missing. "What do you think, angel? Is anything missing?" I turn around to see what she thinks, but as I turn I see that the bastard has passed out. Fuck sake. "Henry, wake up, dickhead. We aren't done yet!" I take the knife from Arlee and stab it into his leg. Henry jolts awake, his head whips side to side, trying to figure out what's going on.

His eyes fill with tears as he tries to look at Arlee with a begging face, but with missing his tongue, an eye, and the knife embedded into his leg, he looks fucking ridiculous. He is on his last legs, *poor guy*.

"Good morning, Sunshine. Before you die, I want you to know that I left the best part for last and I want to see what you think of my fucking tree. Look!" I shout, kicking his chair around to make him look at the tree. While he is facing this way, I grab one of the candy canes and unwrap it.

I turn my attention back to Arlee, her eyes wandering over me like a predatory, hungry for sex. What a greedy little thing.

I stalk up to her and place my index finger under her chin, resting my thumb on her bottom lip. "Open up, angel." I purr, watching as she melts under my touch, following my demands like the good girl she is, her mouth opens wide. I smile and slide the candy cane in her mouth. "Good girl." I whisper into her ear, a shameless moan slips through her throat, making my dick throb.

I look past her and back at Henry, who is jumping in and out of consciousness. I slap the back of his chair as I walk around him. "What's missing? Can you even see?" I chuckle, knowing he probably can't see jack shit with all the blinding pain, well and the fact that he has one eye.

His head wobbles around like a fucking bobblehead on a car dash. Fuck, he is pissing me off.

"Well, I think that one it's missing blood. There are so many souvenirs on here but no blood. What kind of torture tree would it be without blood of the victim." I can't help the excitement I am getting from this and from the excitement I get from Arlee, watching her tease me with the candy cane while we torture her abusive husband. "But second, there aren't enough candy canes on there yet, so I was thinking why not do both, you know kill two birds with one stone." I shrug, walking around behind him, ignoring him for now so I can admire his gorgeous wife.

"Am I distracting you, Hunter?" Her words send

shivers down to my dick, making my pants very uncomfortable to wear.

"I can answer that in like five minutes." I reach around and fist her short hair, pulling her head back to expose her neck to me. "First, I need that candy cane." I breathe on her neck, watching the goosebumps appear on her exposed skin before drifting my tongue across her.

"Hunter, let me?" She begs, I look up from her neck and the look in her eyes make me want to fuck her over this table right here. But, I should at least get rid of this issue before ravishing her. "Can I do it? I made a promise to him."

"Sure, angel." I let her hair go and slam my lips on hers, enjoying her a little before she turns me on fully by going bat shit crazy on her husband.

"So, this is probably going to be fucking painful for you, but so fucking satisfying for me." Arlee calls out to Henry, still looking at me. I unwillingly let her go and my body begs for her to stay, but she needs this. She needs to be the one to do it to move on, to be able to live her life with no fear.

The end of the candy cane is now razor sharp, the point of it glistens in the minimal light of the room. Henry squirms in his seat, trying to make one final attempt at escaping, but he has nothing now. No energy, no family, nothing. I laugh so loudly at his attempt that it scares the literally shit out of him.

"Fuck sake, Henry. Be a man about the situation, please." I slap his face and shake my head.

Arlee stands in front of him, her anger releasing itself. "You want to be the big man, hmm? Hit and abuse your wife. Making your child look after her injured mother for years. Now it's time to accept that Santa's taking your family and will look after them, fucking your wife and making our child his! Have fun with our buddy, Lucifer, tell him I say hi." With that, Arlee rams the sharp end of the candy cane through his jugular, right into his adam's apple. Blood squirts all over the place, but I feel fucking amazing. The blood covered angel that is looking at me now only makes me more turned on, I couldn't be prouder of her.

Arlee lets go of the candy cane and stands high in front of him, wanting to watch the life in his eyes fade away into nothing. Just like he is, nothing!

"Now, my sweet angel, let's go upstairs and shower. I have a gift for you." I take her by the hand and leave Henry there, letting my men deal with him.

Chapter 17

Arlee

THE HOT WATER sends soothing chills down my cold skin, how did I do that? The memories of me killing Henry, finally freeing myself and Gracie completely from his grip. I did that, I can't believe it. The agonising, soundless screams of Henry trying to escape my grip as I popped his eye out, or the look in his eye when I put him out of his misery. What am I? Have I become a monster myself?

"Angel?" Hunter's deep voice blows all the harsh words out of my head, leaving it filled with love and need. "How are you holding up in there? Gracie is asking to see you." His voice softens as Gracie's name leaves his mouth, she has really left a mark on everyone here.

"I'm okay, I'll be out in a second." I call out, turning the water off now that there isn't any hot water left. I step out of the shower and quickly dry myself, throwing on my fresh clothes. The dress Hunter gave me is similar to the one I wore at the Santa pictures, but this one is a lot nicer, the fabric is softer and the colours pop out better against my pale skin.

I take a deep breath in after finishing my hair and makeup and open the door to see Gracie patiently waiting right at the door.

"Hi, Mummy!" Gracie excitedly whispers, her hands clutching together at her chest and her face looks like it's about to explode.

"Hi, baby. Are you okay?" I crouch down to her height, pushing back the short strands out of my face and behind my ear.

"I have a surprise for you." She whispers, jumping up and down gently. "But you have to close your eyes." She demands, no longer jumping around, she's gone into full serious mode.

"Oh, okay." I giggle, standing up and closing my eyes.

Her little giggles are all I hear as she slips her tiny hands into mine, leading me out of the bedroom. We walk around the apartment for what feels like forever before Gracie's hand slips out of mine. Her little feet pat along the wooden floors with her giggles fading away as she goes to who knows where.

"Okay, Mummy! Open your eyes!" She shouts from across the room.

"SURPRISE!" Everyone shouts as I open my eyes, all laughing and cheering in celebration. I laugh and gesture Gracie to come to me so I can cuddle her, needing to transfer this overwhelming amount of joy to my baby.

As she runs into my arms, I stand and take in the view. What was Hunter's apartment decorated with Gracie's birthday party stuff, is now our apartment, fully decked out with Christmas decorations. The roof trim is lined with a beautiful blue tinsel with pieces of pine through it, making it look like the snowy pine trees overseas during this season.

The walls are filled with all different types of hanging decorations and stickers, from Santa to baubles and candy cane stickers. Then, right in the centre of the lounge room, is the Christmas tree. It's exploding with decorations, probably thanks to Gracie. It is huge, standing at two metres with its frosted tips peeking through the heavy amounts of tinsel wrapped around it. The baubles are red, green, silver and white and there is a big golden star right at the top with three little angels sitting at the base of it.

My heart swells as I take in the gorgeous view, I can't hold back the tears that are now rolling down my face.

"Merry Christmas, Mummy!" Gracie squeezes me tightly before running back over to all her friends. I stand and look at her, finally happy to have people that we both can lean on.

"Merry Christmas, baby." I mumble to myself, letting my built up tears fall.

I walk over to the kitchen to grab some water, hopefully to get rid of the massive lump in my throat. We have lost so much, yet we have gained so much.

"Merry Christmas, angel." Hunter's arms slither around my waist, pulling me into him and letting my thoughts slip away into nothing but bliss. "You doing okay?"

"Yeah, just… can't believe Henry's gone." I spin in his arms and pull him into me, resting my head on his chest.

"I know, but you are free and so is Gracie. If you need anything, tell me okay? I'm at your disposal now." Hunter's grin lights up the darkness in my stomach, making it burn away into joy.

"Thank you, Hunter. For everything, I wouldn't be here without you." He leans down and kisses my forehead before leaving me to go to our room.

I look back over at Gracie and all the children,

knowing that I have the best gift of all. A happy family and a happy surprise for everyone.

"Ho ho ho, merry christmas!" Hunter comes out of the bedroom fully dressed in the same Santa outfit from the photo shoot. I hold back my giggle as all the kids jump up and all fall into awe over Santa showing up. "Who's ready for presents!"

WE SPEND all morning going through presents, one by one handing them out to each person around the tree. Wrapping paper tearing and flying all over the place while laughter and happy tears fill the air.

"Well, looks like I am needed at the next house, have a jolly good christmas everyone!" Hunter belly laughs and leaves back through to our bedroom while all the kids giggle and run out of the apartment to play with their toys.

I turn and follow behind him, opening and closing the door quickly behind me so no one sees him changing.

"Hunter." I say, taking a deep breath before walking over to him. He turns on the spot, standing half out of the costume and his hat and beard are still on his face, making me giggle. "Well, aren't you just sexy looking." I can't help but laugh now as he poses in different ways. His muscles flexing with each pose, sending my insides to do backflips.

"Glad you think so, angel." He laughs, fully changing into his normal black shirt and shorts. "Are you okay?" His eyebrows pull together, knowing that something is up with me.

"Am I that easy to read?" My short strands pull in front of my face, concealing the nervous feeling trying to unveil itself.

"A little." Hunter walks over and pushes the strands

back, cupping my cheek as my hair sits behind my ear. "What's wrong?"

"I have a surprise for you." I lower my voice, panic surges through me, hoping that he will be happy. I pull a little box from out of my bedside drawer and hand it to him.

Hunter looks up at me, still with his eyebrows pulled in confusion and unties the bow. He pauses for a moment before lifting the lid off and then freezes, taking in the items inside.

"You're-you are…" His eyes are building out of his head as he flicks between me and the items inside the box. A massive grin appears through his confusion and tears fill his gorgeous brown eyes. "You're pregnant?"

I nod at him with a smile and tears already falling down my face, covering my mouth with both hands so I don't explode. He throws the box on the bed and rushes over to me, picking me up in a hug and spins us around the room.

"It's still early, I would only be a few weeks pregnant-"

"Arlee, that's amazing! I'm-I'm going to be a dad?" Hunter's face couldn't be more happy if he tried. The watery streaking lingering on his face and the huge smile he can't seem to get rid of fills my heart.

"Well, I would say you're Gracie's dad, but yes." He shrieks like a little girl and picks me up again. Taking a moment to fully absorb the information, he looks back at the box before running out of the room.

"I'm going to be a dad!" He shouts, running through our apartment and out the door, finding all his friends to celebrate with.

Epilogue

Ace

10 months later

HALLOWEEN DECORATIONS ARE HANGING all over the outside of our building. Skeletons and graves in the front facing the parking lot and spider webs are scattering the trees. The back has themed lights and a few hanging decorations about, but with our graveyard out here, we don't let many come out here.

I walk through the outdoor play area we have fenced and open the gate to the cemetery, where all of our crew get buried after they pass. All family, blood or bond, knows where they are if they wish to visit. I walk through the lines of different size graves, all with a different quote or saying written across it. The sinking feeling of my heart hits as I walk closer and closer to his resting place.

Talon's funeral was almost a year ago, and not one day goes by that I don't think about him. The way he would soften around me, the bond we had, being brothers, is something that I will never have again. Not in the same way.

His grave stone stands tall down the back, being the most recent member we have lost. His stone reads,

Family isn't bounded by only blood, but in the bonds that you make along the way. Wait for us up there with a cold one. Rest well, brother.

James 'Talon' Barden

I bend down and place down a small bouquet of flowers the kids picked from our front gardens in front of his stone. Tears build in my eyes as guilt washes over me, knowing that it's all my fault he's gone.

"Hey, brother. How are you doing?" I sniffle, wishing that he could actually answer me. "I'm doing good, works been great with Henry gone. Our company is thriving. The crew's doing well, we have had a few new additions amongst the crew. They are still doing initiation training, but one of them reminds me of us when we were his age." I chuckle to myself, a tear slowly dragging its way down my face.

"Umm, what else?" I take a deep breath and look down at the small child strapped to my chest, his gorgeous blue eyes staring up at me. "I thought it was about time you met my son, James." The tears no longer stay where they should and streak my face, falling onto the ground at Talon's feet. "I wish you could have met him, man. He's amazing." I slowly sit on the ground in front of the stone, taking James out of the carrier. "Look at him, isn't he adorable?"

I can feel him here, looking at my first son with so much happiness in his heart. I can't help but break down over the thought. As I try to kiss James forehead, he makes a small happy sound and grabs my finger, my breathing freezes. "Talon…" The word almost coming out as a sob, can James feel him too, watching us? I lean down and kiss his forehead, planting my lips gently on his skin before putting him back into his carrier to let him sleep.

"Arlee and Gracie are doing amazing too. Angel was so strong during the birth. I could feel you beside me while I waited, you know. Your hand on my shoulder, whispers in my ear saying how great I'll be and that I'm nothing like my dad so I have nothing to worry about." I wipe my snotty nose and chuckle to myself over how soft I've got. "Gracie's thriving, she asks about you all the time, wishing she could come visit you. I don't think she fully understands that you're not…" My words turn to ash on my tongue while my eyes pour more tears out. "She misses you bro. We all do." I flick my tears away and stand back up, looking down at James and then at Talon's grave.

"Come on, James. It's time for you to have some food." I sniffle again, taking one last look at Talon before I leave him to rest.

I know he will watch over us, he has always been a guardian. Someone who will do whatever it takes to look after his family, he did that for me and that's what got him killed.

"Wait for me, I want to punch you for leaving me so soon." I shout over my shoulder and rub my hand on James' back. Trying to comfort myself through him, looking at his little face that looks just like mine.

I walk out of the grave and know that he's here, walking alongside me to come and watch over everyone. The same as he did while he was still breathing. It's not the same though, knowing that I can't talk to him and get a response, or tell him I'll shove him in my sack for making fun of me. All that is gone, but the memories will be treasured forever.

www.ingramcontent.com/pod-product-compliance
Lightning Source LLC
LaVergne TN
LVHW051012080826
845145LV00009B/2577

* 9 7 8 1 7 6 4 2 1 1 3 3 8 *